A Prisoner of Mo
Hands of th

Upton Sinclair

Alpha Editions

This edition published in 2024

ISBN 9789362516329

Design and Setting By
Alpha Editions
www.alphaedis.com
Email - info@alphaedis.com

Contents

CHAPTER I.

SIGHTING A PRIZE.

About noon of a day in May during the recent year the converted tug Uncas left Key West to join the blockading squadron off the northern coast of Cuba.

Her commander was Lieutenant Raymond, and her junior officer Naval Cadet Clifford Faraday. The regular junior officer was absent on sick leave, and Cadet Faraday had been assigned to his place in recognition of gallant conduct.

The ropes were cast off, and slowly the tug glided away from the dock and out toward the open sea.

It was not very long before the harbor of Key West was left behind, and then began the long trip to Havana. It was over a hundred miles, and that meant seven or eight hours' journey for the Uncas.

But the Uncas was a good, stout vessel, unusually swift for a tug, and she made the water fairly fly when once she got clear of the land.

Clif leaned against one of the rapid-firing guns in the bow and gazed longingly ahead; he was anxious to reach his destination.

There were wild rumors concerning Spanish fleets, Cadiz squadrons and Cape Verde squadrons and Mediterranean squadrons, which were continually being sighted or heard of nearby; and for all Clif knew the decisive battle of the war might be fought at any time.

And he felt that if it took place while he was absent he would never cease to regret it as long as he lived. The Uncas could not do much in such a battle; but she was anxious to do her share.

It was possible, also, that Morro might succeed in provoking an attack. The guns of the Havana defenses kept blazing away at anything that came near, and the American sailors were fairly boiling over with impatience to get a whack at them.

And at any time Admiral Sampson might give the word.

So Clif was restless and impatient as he stood in the bow of the swift tug and gazed southward.

It was a rather damp place of observation the cadet had chosen, for it had been blowing quite a gale that day, and the Uncas was plowing her way through a heavy sea.

The spray was flying over the decks; but who would have thought of going below at such a time as that?

It was not Clif's turn on duty. Lieutenant Raymond seemed to think that after his struggle on board the Spanish monitor the young cadet deserved a rest. But he was too eager and wide awake just then to wish to take it.

When the tug was well under way the lieutenant came out of the pilot house and joined Clif again.

"Thinking of the weather, Mr. Faraday?" inquired Lieutenant Raymond.

"No, sir," replied the cadet, "I was thinking of Ignacio. I don't know how he happened to get into my thoughts, but he did."

"Who is Ignacio?"

"He's a Spaniard I've had some trouble with," answered Clif. "You may have heard about one of his exploits."

"Which one is that?"

"He made an attempt to assassinate Rear Admiral Sampson."

"Oh, yes, I heard about that," said the officer. "The admiral told me about it himself. I believe you were the person who interfered."

"I had the good luck to be standing near," said Clif, modestly. "And of course, I sprang between them."

"And the spy stabbed you?"

"Yes. In the shoulder, but he did not hurt me very much."

"He must be a desperate man."

"He is. That stabbing business seems to be a favorite trick of his. I hope I shan't have to face him again."

Whether Ignacio was a Spaniard or a traitor Cuban, no one could say. Clif had first met him trying to lead astray an American officer who had been sent with dispatches for Gomez.

And Clif had foiled the plot, and had been Ignacio's deadly enemy ever since. Clif had been keeping a careful watch for him. He knew that the vindictive fellow would follow his every move; Ignacio was acting as a spy for the Spaniards, and so must have found it easy to keep track of the cadet's whereabouts. But so far Clif had not met him.

"We are likely to have a wild night of it," said Lieutenant Raymond. "The clouds seem to get darker every minute."

"It'll be a night for the blockade-runners," was Clif's answer. "We may have some excitement."

"We'll have it anyway," said the other. "I don't know of anything I less rather do than weather a storm while in among the vessels of the fleet. It will be necessary to stay on deck every instant of the time keeping watch for our very lives."

"I know how it is," the cadet added. "I was on the Porter dining one such night. And we captured a prize coming out of Havana after almost running her down in the darkness."

"I heard about it," said Lieutenant Raymond. "You may repeat the performance to-night if you have a chance. We aren't likely to meet with anything till we get there."

As the lieutenant said that he turned and gazed ahead; the broad sea stretched out on every side of them, without a sign of smoke or sail to vary the monotony of its tossing waves.

"But it always lends zest to a trip like this," the officer added, "to know that it's possible you may run across a stray Spaniard at any moment. It pays to keep one's eyes open."

"And then you have the pleasure of chasing two or three and finding they're some other nation's ships," said Clif, with a laugh.

"That's about all we've done so far," said the lieutenant. "But we're still hoping perhaps you'll bring us good luck."

"I'll do my best," the cadet declared with a smile.

"Better get ready for it by resting a bit. Your dinner's ready below."

Clif took the hint and went below. The boat was pitching so violently that he found eating a very difficult operation, and it was generally so unpleasant in the little cabin that he was glad to go on deck again.

And then later in the afternoon, at four o'clock, it came time for him to go on duty. After that he had to remain outside whether he wanted to or not.

The gale grew considerably stronger, and as the darkness came on it got much chillier, but Clif still paced up and down the deck with the glass in his hand watching for a sign of a passing vessel, or of the approaching Cuban coast.

He was left almost alone on deck as the weather got rougher; for the crew made themselves comfortable below, knowing what hard work lay before them through the stormy night.

It was not the custom on the vessel to keep the whole watch on duty except at night; and Clif had only the two sailors at the wheel and the lookout in the bow for company.

But if he felt any jealousy of those who were below out of the cold, he had the grim satisfaction of being able to disturb their comfort before very long.

It was about half past four in the afternoon, and suddenly the lookout turned and called to Clif.

The eager cadet knew what it meant. He seized the glass and hurried forward.

He followed the direction of the man's finger.

"I think I see smoke, sir," was what the sailor said.

And Clif took a long look and then turned, his face betraying his excitement.

An instant later his voice rang through the ship.

"Steamer ahoy—off the starboard bow!"

CHAPTER II.

A LONG CHASE.

There was excitement on board of the Uncas the instant Clif's cry was heard. The sailors came tumbling up on deck, Lieutenant Raymond among the first.

He took the glass eagerly from the lad's hand and anxiously studied the sky in the direction indicated.

"It's too far west to be near Havana!" he exclaimed.

And he stepped into the pilot house to direct the vessel in a new direction. At the same time the smoke began to pour from the funnel, showing that those down in the engine-room had heard Clif's hail.

And so in a few moments the Uncas was speeding away in the direction of the stranger. And after that there was a long weary wait while the two vessels gradually drew nearer.

All that could be made out then was the long line of smoke which always indicates a distant steamer. But it took a sharp eye to make even that out.

"This will be a long chase," said the lieutenant. "If she takes it into her head to run we'll have a hard time to catch up to her before dark."

Clif glanced significantly at the bow gun.

"If we can only get within range," he thought to himself, "we won't have to wait to catch up to her."

The lieutenant was standing by the pilot house with the glass in his hand, and every once in a while he would make an attempt to catch sight of the stranger's smokestack.

"It may be one of our own warships," he said, "and if it is we don't want to waste any coal chasing her."

But such was not the case, and it was only half an hour or so before the lieutenant found it out. The Uncas rose as a high wave swept by; and the officer, who had the glass to his eye, gave an eager exclamation.

"She's got one funnel," he exclaimed, "and it's black, with a red top; and so it's not an American warship."

And after that there was nothing now to be done except wait until the two approached nearer.

It was evident from the gradual change of course the Uncas was obliged to make that the vessel she was following was headed in a southerly direction.

"That would take her toward the western end of Cuba," Clif thought to himself. "Perhaps she's sighted us and is running away."

She must have been a very shy vessel to have taken alarm at so great a distance; but from the slowness with which she came into view that seemed to be the case. And Clif paced the deck impatiently.

It was not very much longer before he went off duty again; but he did not go below. For perhaps an hour he remained on deck watching the strange vessel.

It seemed an age, but Clif had his reward. The chase loomed gradually nearer. The black and red smoke pipe came into view, and then, when the Uncas rose, the top of the black hull as well.

And suddenly the lieutenant handed the glass to Clif.

"You may see now," he said. "She is a merchant steamer, and she flies the Spanish flag."

Clif nearly dropped the glass at those startling words. The lieutenant said them as calmly as if he were telling the time of day.

"You don't seem very much excited," the cadet thought.

And yet the lieutenant's statement proved to be true. It was several minutes before Clif got a favorable view; but he kept his eyes fixed on the smoke and he finally caught a glimpse of the hull.

And sure enough there was the hated red and yellow ensign waving defiantly from the stern; it was blown off to one side by the breeze, and could be plainly seen.

Clif was fairly boiling over with excitement at that discovery.

"We've got our prize!" he chuckled. "I brought the luck after all."

Lieutenant Raymond was not nearly so little moved as he chose to pretend; he had announced his discovery in that careless way half in a spirit of fun.

The news got round among the crew, and however the officer may have felt, there was no indifference there.

The engines of the Uncas began to work even more rapidly, and cartridges were hastily brought up for the rapid-firing guns. Nobody meant to let that steamer get away.

She must have suspected her danger by that time, for the smoke grew blacker. But the crew of the Uncas knew that there were few merchant ships could beat that tug, and they rubbed their hands gleefully.

There is something very aggravating about a race like that. In a rowing race you may break your back if you choose, trying to catch the boat in front; and even in a sailing race you may do something. But when it comes to steam you can only grit your teeth and walk up and down and watch and try not to let anybody see how anxious you are.

In that way half an hour passed away, and mile after mile of the storm-tossed waters.

By that time the hull of the vessel was plainly visible on the horizon; and the Spanish flag was still waving from her stern.

Clif had been gazing every once in a while at the lieutenant with an inquiring look upon his face, but the officer had only shaken his head.

"Not yet," he said. "Wait a little."

And Clif would then take another stroll across the deck.

But at last his inquiring look brought another answer.

"Go ahead," said the lieutenant.

And the cadet made a leap at the gun.

It was already loaded, and he sighted it himself. He was no longer nervous and hurried; it was at least a minute before he rose.

And then at his signal the sailor pulled the firing trigger.

There was a flash and a loud report, and every one looked anxiously to see the effect.

Lieutenant Raymond, who had the glass, was the only one who could tell; for the sea was so wild that the slight splash could not be noticed.

The shot of course fell short, for the vessel was still out of range; but it hit right in line, and the officer nodded approvingly.

"Now we'll wait," he said. "She may give up."

But she didn't; so far as those on the Uncas could tell the shot had no effect whatever. The vessel kept straight on in her course.

"She's counting on the darkness coming," said the lieutenant.

But that was not the only reason why the Spaniard did not give up; those upon the Uncas discovered another shortly afterward.

"The Cuban coast," exclaimed the officer.

Yes, the long, faint line of the shore was at last visible just on the horizon's edge. It lay to the southward, directly ahead.

"What good will that do her?" asked Clif.

"If she finds she can't get away," answered the other, "she may make a run for one of the ports or try to get under the shelter of the batteries."

For a while after that nothing more was said, and the tug plowed its way through the tossing water. When the lieutenant spoke again it was to point to the gun.

"Try it again," he said.

And Clif did try it. The two ships were then not over three or four miles apart, and when the cadet fired again he heard the lieutenant give a pleased exclamation.

"They're within range!"

And then Clif got to work with all his might.

Had he had a calm sea he could have raked that vessel without missing a shot. He had only to experiment and get the aim just right and then leave the gun to stay in that one position while he blazed away.

But the Uncas in climbing over the waves was now up and now down, so that sometimes the shots fell short and sometimes they went high.

But every once in a while he had the satisfaction of hearing that he had landed one.

After that the chase was a lively one, for the Uncas kept blazing away merrily. The people on board that fleeing vessel must have had a very large time of it that afternoon.

It was just what Clif Faraday liked; he was beginning to be quite an expert in target practice, and he was willing to experiment with that ship just as long as the ammunition held out.

But his opportunity did not last very long, for the land in front was neared very rapidly, and after that there was less fun and more work.

The stranger headed round gradually to the west. She evidently had no idea of being driven toward Havana.

The Uncas swerved more sharply, in order to head her off. Lieutenant Raymond was in the pilot house, and Clif soon saw by the way he managed things that he was an expert in all the tricks of dodging.

And those who were handling the merchant ship saw it, too; they would have been soon headed off. So they turned in another direction quite sharply, making straight in toward shore again.

Under ordinary circumstances with the short range that he had by that time, Clif could have riddled the vessel in short order; but aiming in that sea was so far a matter of luck that comparatively little damage could be done.

No one knew what the enemy's last move could mean.

"But we can go in any water that's deep enough for them," thought Clif, grimly, as he blazed away.

And so thought the lieutenant, too, for he was soon racing in. For perhaps ten minutes pursuer and pursued kept straight on, the firing never ceasing for a moment.

"Perhaps she may run on shore on purpose," said the lieutenant, coming out of the pilot house for a moment.

"On purpose?" echoed Clif.

"Yes; so that we can't get the cargo."

"But she'll be beaten to pieces on the rocks," Clif objected.

"They may chance it anyhow; you see they aren't more than a mile or two from the shore now, and they're running in still."

"If that's the trick they try," Clif thought to himself, "we can stay out and pepper her to our heart's content—and help the waves to wreck her."

But the Spaniard had a far better plan than that, as her pursuers learned some time later.

Clif studied the coast in front of them, as well as he could see without a glass; there was simply a long line of sandy shore without a bay or an inlet of any kind. And there were no towns or batteries visible.

"I don't see what she can be hoping for there," he muttered.

But he had no time to speculate in the matter, for it was his business to keep firing. By that time the range was short and he was beginning to do damage.

It took an expert to fire at the instant when the tossing ship was level, but Clif had time to practice, and he soon got the knack of it.

And then it must have been exceedingly unpleasant living on that ship. One after another the heavy six-pound shots crashed through her stern; and even at that distance it began to exhibit a ragged appearance.

The cadet expected at any moment to reach the engines or the rudder of the fleeing ship, and so render her helpless. But probably her cargo served to protect the former, and the rudder was very hard to hit.

"She must have something important in view to stand all this," Clif thought to himself. "But I can't see what it is."

The chase at that time was a very exciting one. The Spanish merchantman was dashing in shore at the top of his speed. And a mile or two beyond it was the Uncas tearing up the water, plunging along at her fastest pace and banging away half a dozen times a minute with her bow gun.

Lieutenant Raymond's eyes were dancing then; he had taken the wheel himself and was hard at work. And as for Clif, he was so busily engaged that he seemed to see nothing except the high stern of that runaway.

"But she's a fool," he growled to himself. "She'll be so torn to pieces she won't be worth capturing. I wish I could kill the captain."

But the captain of that vessel knew his business, as those on the Uncas found later on. He was a Spaniard, and simply gifted with Spanish cunning.

He had no idea of running his ship aground; but he knew that coast perfectly, and he used his knowledge.

When he neared the land the tug was still some distance astern. As that did not suit the Spaniard's purposes, he very calmly slowed up.

And that in spite of the fact that the tug was so close that the rapid-firing gun was hitting him every other shot!

That the vessel had slowed up, Lieutenant Raymond of course could not tell. But he wouldn't have cared anyhow, for he had made up his mind to go in there no matter what was there, torpedoes or the very Old Nick himself.

And he went; for perhaps five minutes more the Uncas dashed in at full speed, and the merchantman still never swerved.

"They're within a quarter of a mile of the shore!" gasped Clif.

He turned to his third box of cartridges with a grim smile on his face. For he knew that something must happen soon.

It did, too—very soon.

It began when the merchantman suddenly swung round to starboard.

"Aha!" chuckled the cadet. "They're as close in as they dare. And now I suppose they'll run down shore awhile."

Lieutenant Raymond was much puzzled to think why the vessel had risked going so close in that storm; but he wasted no time in speculating, but drove the wheel around with all his might.

The Uncas swerved and sped over to shut the merchantman off; at that same instant the reason of the whole thing was seen.

The Uncas was not a mile from shore, and as she turned her broadside to the land a masked battery in the sand let drive with a dozen guns at once.

The whole thing was so sudden that for a moment it quite frightened the Americans. Clif even stopped firing long enough to stare.

But the sudden alarm did not last very long; it left the men on the Uncas laughing. For they had quite forgotten the character of the Spanish gunners' aim.

A shot tore through the tug's funnel, another chipped a piece from her bow, half a dozen shells whistled over her. And that was all.

Clif turned calmly to his gun again.

"If that's the best they can do," he thought, "they're welcome."

But that was not the best.

It wasn't that the batteries were aimed better next time. They were aimed far worse in their eager haste. They did not even touch the Uncas.

But an instant later something happened that showed that the captain of the Spanish merchantman had one more string to his bow.

He not only knew the location of the batteries, but he knew the location of the sand bars. While his own vessel sped on in safety, on board the Uncas there suddenly came a grinding thud, and an instant later the tug stopped short, so short it almost sent Clif flying over the top of the gun he was working.

And at the same time a shout was heard from Lieutenant Raymond, one that made the sailors' hearts leap up into their throats: "We're aground! We're aground!"

And in front of a Spanish battery!

CHAPTER III.

AN OLD ENEMY.

It would be hard to imagine a vessel in a much greater predicament than the Uncas was at that moment. Everything was in confusion in an instant.

That is everything except one thing. Lieutenant Raymond was too busy to notice the coolness of one person on board; but he remembered it afterward, and with satisfaction.

It was Clif Faraday; he picked himself up from the deck where he had been flung and took one glance about him. Then he turned to the guns.

Whatever the position of the tug his duty just then remained the same. He could not free her, and so he did not waste any time rushing about. There was that Spanish merchantman calmly walking off to safety.

And there was a gleam of vengeance in the cadet's eye as he went to the gun again.

Those on board of the fleeing vessel had seen the success of their clever plan and they gave a wild cheer. It was answered from the shore batteries.

The steamer turned at once and headed out to sea; that put her broadside to the Uncas, and instantly the six-pounder blazed away.

That was the time to do the work, too. The vessel was quite near, and a fair mark. The Uncas was now steady, too, Clif thought grimly to himself.

One of the sailors saw what he was doing, and sprang to aid him. They banged away as fast as they could load.

At the same time the Spanish batteries opened. They had a fair mark, likewise, and plenty of time to aim. It was a race to see who could smash up their prey the quickest.

Clif would certainly have disabled the fleeing vessel if it had not been for an unfortunate accident. What the accident was may be told in a few words. It spoiled his chance.

He turned away to get more cartridges. And at that instant a shell struck the six-pounder gun.

It was a miracle that Clif was not hit; his uniform was torn in three places and his cap knocked off. The sailor next to him got a nasty wound in the arm, made by a flying fragment.

And that of course made the merchantman safe—she steamed off in triumph.

It was bad for the tug, too, for it showed the batteries were getting the range.

The plight of the Uncas was a desperate one. She was being tossed about by a raging sea and cut up by the fire from the guns. Whether she had struck on rocks or sand or mud no one had any means of telling.

But her engines were reversed the instant the accident occurred. And a hasty examination of the hold showed that whatever the danger was there was no leak.

But that seemed cold comfort, for at the rate the heavy batteries were blazing away there was likely to be a number of leaks in a very short while. And even a steel tug will not hold together long with a sea pounding over her like this one was.

Yet as it actually happened, that sea was the only thing that got the vessel out of her unfortunate predicament.

They were a great deal luckier than they would have dared to hope to be. For when they realized they were aground there was not a man on board who did not think his last hour was at hand.

But as it actually happened, the sand bar upon which the tug had driven lay some distance beneath the surface. And it had caught the vessel by the keel.

The engines throbbed wildly, doing their noblest to pull the vessel off; and then one after another came the great waves, tossing her this way and that, wrenching and twisting, lifting and lifting again, while every one on deck clung for his life.

There was a minute or two of agonizing suspense, while the shore batteries kept up a galling fire and the merchantman steamed out to sea, proud of her triumph.

And then suddenly came a wild cheer from the imperiled Americans. Then men fairly shrieked in a transport of delight.

"She's moving! She's started! She's safe!"

And the men fairly hugged each other for joy. Slowly, then faster, then faster still, and finally at full speed backward. The gallant tug had torn herself loose from the grip of the sand—and was free!

The baffled Spanish batteries redoubled their fire at that. One could almost imagine the gunners grinding their teeth with rage as they saw their prey escaping.

But grinding their teeth did not seem to sharpen their eyes. Their aim was as bad as ever, and the Uncas seemed like the proverbial man in the rainstorm who keeps dry by "dodging the drops."

The confusion on board of the "escaped" vessel may be imagined. How that triumphant captain must have sworn Spanish oaths.

It was a ticklish task that Lieutenant Raymond had before him then. He knew there were sand bars about. But he did not know where they were. And the task was to avoid them.

He did it by creeping along very slowly, in absolute indifference to the galling fire from the shore guns. He knew that there must be a channel, for he and the Spaniard had come in by it.

He had only a vague idea where it was. But the Uncas stopped and then crept slowly forward, heading north.

And after five minutes of torment they knew that they were safe. They were far enough from shore to start up again and get away from those Spanish guns. The gallant tug was quite battered by that time, but nobody cared for that in the wild rejoicing that prevailed.

The vessel swung around to port.

"And now for that prize!" muttered the lieutenant.

And he went for her, too, full speed ahead. He was mad now.

The vessel had gotten a start of about two miles. She had apparently exhausted her resources in the neighborhood of Cuba, for she was heading north, out to sea again.

"And so it's only a question of time," chuckled Clif. "We've got her!"

And so they had. The Spaniards must have realized it, too.

"Mr. Faraday," said the lieutenant, "try a shot from the starboard gun."

The shot was fired; and it did the work.

The merchantman had evidently had enough, and saw that there was no further hope.

For in full view of the shore batteries she swung round and came slowly to a halt, a signal that she surrendered. It made the Americans give another cheer, and it must have made the Spaniards on shore fairly yell.

For they began banging away, even at that distance, though they couldn't come anywhere near the tug.

As for the Americans, they sighed with relief. They had worked hard for that victory. And they felt that they had earned it. The race was over then, and they were happy.

Clif was so wearied by his heroic labor at that gun (he must have lifted and rammed some two hundred six-pounder cartridges) that he sat down on the wreck of the machine to wait until the two vessels drew near.

And the lieutenant gave up the wheel to one of the men and came out to look his capture over at leisure.

She was a fairly large vessel and seemed to have a big carrying capacity. What she was loaded with no one could guess, but at any rate she was a big prize for a small crew like that of the Uncas.

"I think I'll retire from business after to-day," Clif heard the old boatswain remark.

That personage had had one arm badly damaged in the struggle that had taken place in the morning with the Spanish gunboat; but he seemed to have forgotten his wounds in the general excitement.

The little tug steamed up boldly toward her big prize, which lay idly tossing on the waves. One could see her officers and crew standing on deck watching the approach.

"I'll bet they feel happy!" Clif muttered to himself.

The lieutenant loaned him the glass. Then he could see the faces of the men.

There was one of them he might have recognized had he been careful; but he did not recognize it, and so he failed to save himself some mighty unpleasant adventures indeed.

They were all typical Spanish faces, dark and sullen; but there was one there even darker and more sullen than the rest.

And the owner of that countenance had a glass in his hand and was staring at those on the tug. Though the cadet did not know it, that man was at that instant watching him.

And there was an expression of furious hate on his face as he looked.

Lieutenant Raymond expected no further trouble; but he took no chances. Men were stationed at the three remaining six-pounders, and the rest of the crew was armed.

In silence the Uncas steamed up to within a hundred yards of her prize. And then came the signal to stop engines.

It was the time for a boarding party. Clif, as junior officer, knew that that was his duty, and without a word he proceeded to get the small boat off.

It was quite a task in that heavy sea, but the eager sailors worked with a will, and though nearly swamped twice, managed to get clear of the tug.

And Clif was seated in the stern, heading for the big merchantman.

"Keep your eyes open," he heard the lieutenant shout. "They may make trouble."

And Clif nodded and the boat shot away. They wouldn't catch him napping on board that Spanish vessel—not much!

But they come perilously near it all the same.

It was a rough trip in that tossing rowboat. It seemed to sink and then fairly bound up on the next wave, its bow went down and its stern shot up. It did everything except turn over, while the spray fairly flew over it.

But the sturdy sailors worked with a will, and the distance was not very great. In a short time the little craft shot round in the lee of the Spaniard.

"A ladder there!" shouted Clif.

And in a few moments the rope ladder came tumbling down. It seemed to come with bad grace though, as if it knew its owners didn't want to send it.

The rowboat was backed near and Clif, with a sudden spring, caught the ladder and leaped clear of the waves.

Before he went up he turned to the sailors.

"Two of you follow me," he commanded.

He climbed quickly up the ladder and stepped out on the deck, gazing about him eagerly.

He saw about a dozen dark-faced Spaniards gathered together and glaring at him; one of them, wearing the uniform of the captain, stepped forward toward him.

He was a surly, ill-looking man, with a heavy dark mustache. He bowed stiffly to the cadet.

"The senor takes possession," he said, in a low voice.

Clif was so busy watching this man that he did not look around the vessel. But we must do so.

We must glance for one instant at the capstan, which was just behind where the jaunty young cadet was standing. There was an interesting person near the capstan.

Clif did not see him; and neither did the sailors, nor even the Spaniards on the vessel. For he was crouching behind the capstan, out of sight.

He was a small man, dark and swarthy. He was the same one we noticed glaring at Clif; he had recognized him, and realized in a flash that the issue between them was death—death for one or else death for the other.

For Clif knew the man, and would secure him the instant he saw him; his crimes were many—treason and attempted assassination the worst.

For the man was Ignacio!

And his dark, beady eyes were glittering with hatred as he crouched in his momentary hiding-place. He was quivering all over with rage; the muscles of his sinewy arms were clinched and tense.

And in his right hand he clutched a sharp, gleaming knife, half hidden under his coat.

His glance was fixed on the figure just in front of him; the unsuspecting cadet was not twenty yards away, his back turned to his crouching enemy.

And Ignacio bent forward to listen and wait his chance.

The cadet, the object of his hatred, was talking to the captain.

"The senor takes possession," the latter repeated again.

"The senor does, with your permission," said Clif, quietly.

"You gave us quite a run," he added, after a moment's thought.

"A Spaniard would not surrender to Yankee pigs without a fight," snarled the other.

"You had best be a bit careful," was Clif's stern response, "or you may find yourself in irons."

The Spaniard relapsed into a sullen silence.

"What ship is this?" demanded the cadet.

"The Maria."

"From where?"

"Cadiz."

"Indeed! And bound where?"

"Bahia Honda."

Clif gave a low whistle.

"We caught you about in time," he said, with a smile. "You were nearly there. But I suppose the story is made up for the occasion. What is your cargo?"

The captain went over quite a list of articles; the sailors who were with Clif chuckled with delight as they heard him.

"We get a share in all this," Clif heard one of them whisper under his breath.

Clif smiled; and as soon as the captain finished he raised his arm and pointed to the stern of the vessel.

"You and your men will go aft," he commanded, "for the present; I will see you shortly."

The Spaniard was on the point of obeying; he had half turned, when suddenly with a single bound the treacherous Ignacio sprang forward.

His keen knife glanced in the air as he raised it in his outstretched arm and leaped upon the unsuspecting cadet.

Ignacio was clever at that sort of thing. He had tried it before; his spring had been silent as a cat's. Neither the sailors nor the officer heard him. And the blow might have fallen; Clif's only warning of his deadly peril.

But unfortunately for the desperate assassin, he had failed to let the captain of that vessel know what he meant to do. And the captain, as he saw him leap, realized in a flash that would mean an instant hanging for him.

And a look of horror swept over his face; Clif saw it and whirled about.

He was just in time to find himself face to face with his deadliest enemy; and the knife was hissing through the air.

CHAPTER IV.

IN COMMAND OF THE PRIZE.

It was a moment of horrible peril. Clif's blood fairly froze. But quick as a flash his arm shot up.

And he caught the descending wrist; for an instant the two glared into each other's eyes, straining and twisting. And then the two sailors of the Uncas leaped forward and seized the baffled Spaniard.

And almost in the twinkling of an eye-lid, Clif Faraday was saved. He could hardly realize what had happened, and he staggered back against the railing of the vessel and gasped for breath.

But that was only for a moment, too; and then the blood surged back to his cheeks and the cadet was himself once more.

He stepped forward, a calm smile playing about his mouth.

"Bind that man," he said to the sailors.

The two men were grasping the sinewy Cuban and holding him so tight that he could not move. They almost crushed his wrists, and he dropped the knife with a hoarse cry of pain.

And Clif picked it up and glanced at it for a moment, then flung it far out into the sea.

After that he turned to Ignacio.

"You have met me once more, my friend," he said, "and this time you will not get away."

And that was all the conversation he had with him. Glancing about the deck he picked up a piece of rope and stepped toward the prisoner.

He did not strike the fellow, as the Spaniards seemed to think he would. But the sailors flung him to the deck and Clif carefully bound his feet together. Then, while he fairly fumed with rage and hatred, his hands were made fast and he was left lying there, shrieking curses in his native Spanish.

Clif turned to the captain of the vessel; the man was frightened nearly to death, and began protesting volubly.

"I did not know it, senor!" he cried. "Indeed, I did not know it! Santa Maria! I——"

"I don't suppose you did," said Clif, calmly. "You did not act like it. But you will have to suffer for it."

"Suffer for it! Madre di dios, no, senor! What does the senor mean? Surely he will not hang me for——"

"The senor will not hang you," said Clif, unable to help smiling at the blustering fellow's terror.

"Then what will the senor do?"

"He will tie you like Ignacio."

The man was evidently relieved, but he protested volubly. He did not want to be tied.

"Is it customary?" he cried.

"No," said Clif; "neither is it customary to try to assassinate an officer. After that I think common prudence requires it."

"But," cried the man, angrily. "I will not submit! Por dios, I will not——"

"You will either submit or be made to," said Clif, "or else sink to the bottom."

And so the man had to give up. Those two delighted tars went the rounds and tied every single man on that vessel hand and foot. And they tied them tight, too, occasionally giving them a dig in the ribs for good measure.

And when they came to search them Clif was glad he had done as he did, for quite a respectable heap of knives and revolvers were removed from the clothes of those angry Spaniards.

But it did not take long to tie them up, and then Clif felt safe. He took a few extra hitches in the treacherous Ignacio, who was by far the most valuable prize of them all.

"Admiral Sampson will be glad to get you," the cadet thought to himself.

And then he turned to examine the captured vessel.

His sword in his hand, he went down the forward companionway, where he met a group of frightened firemen and stokers huddled below. They seemed to think the Yankee pigs were going to murder them on the spot.

But Clif had another use for them. Being able to speak Spanish, he found it easy to reassure them in a few words, and sent them down to their work again.

Then he descended into the hold; he was worried lest the continuous firing he had directed upon the vessel had made her unseaworthy. But apparently the holes were all well above the water line, for there did not seem to be any leak.

And that was all there was to be done. Clif knew that he had the task before him of piloting that vessel into Key West; he was not willing to let that ugly-looking Spanish captain have anything to do with the matter.

Clif had fancied he would rather enjoy that duty but under the circumstances of the present case he was not so much pleased.

For the darkness was gathering then and the cadet knew that he had a long hard night before him; it would be necessary for him to remain on the vessel's bridge all through the stormy trip.

And, moreover, it would take him away from Havana, the place of all places he was then anxious to reach.

But the duty had to be faced, and so Clif sent one of the sailors back to the Uncas to report the state of affairs and ask for a prize crew. It seemed scarcely orthodox to send the small boat away without an officer to command it, but that, too, was inevitable.

The boat arrived safely, however, and returned with three more men, all the little tug dared spare. Lieutenant Raymond sent word to report at Key West with the prize, but to steam slowly so as not to come anywhere near the shore before daylight.

Lieutenant Raymond was evidently a little worried about intrusting that big vessel to an inexperienced officer like Clif, and Clif was not so very cock sure himself. No one knew just where they were, and in the storm and darkness reaching Key West harbor would be task enough for an old hand.

The cadet realized the enormous responsibility thus thrown upon him, and he made up his mind that eternal vigilance should be the watchword.

"If staying awake all night'll do any good," he muttered, "I'll do it."

And then the small boat dashed away to the Uncas again, and Clif was left alone. He stepped into the pilot house of the steamer and signaled for half speed ahead.

The vessel began to glide slowly forward again, heading north; the tug steamed away in the direction of Havana.

CHAPTER V.

A HAIL FROM THE DARKNESS.

The four sailors who were with Clif fully realized the task which was before them.

It was then about dusk, and the night was coming on rapidly. Two of the men were stationed as lookouts, and the other two took the wheel.

Clif set to work to try to calculate as best he could how far and in what direction he was from Key West; he wished to take no chances of running ashore or getting lost.

Those, and the possibility of collision, seemed the only dangers that had to be guarded against; the possibility of meeting a Spanish vessel was not considered, for the chance seemed very remote.

The two lookouts were both stationed in the bow. That fact and the other just mentioned sufficed to account for the fact that the real danger that threatened the crew of the merchantman was not thought of or guarded against in the least.

For Clif had no way of knowing that any trouble was to come from behind him; but coming it was, and in a hurry.

Within the shelter of a narrow inlet just to one side of the batteries that had made so much trouble for the Uncas had lain hidden and unsuspected an object that was destined to play an important part in the rest of the present story.

It was a Spanish gunboat, of much the same kind as the Uncas, only smaller. Hidden by the land, her officers had eagerly watched the struggle we have just seen.

The Spanish vessel had not ventured out to take part, for one important reason; she had not steam up. But she would probably not have done so anyhow, for the Uncas was the stronger of the two.

And so venturing out would have been little better than suicide. The Spanish captain had a plan that put that one far in the shade.

The Uncas was still visible down the shore, and the merchantman had hardly gotten well started out to sea before great volumes of black smoke began to pour from the furnaces of the Spaniard.

Her men worked like fiends; sailors pitched in to help the firemen handle coal, while the shores of the dark little inlet flared brightly with the gleam of the furnaces.

Meanwhile the officers with their glasses were feverishly watching the distant steamer, now hull down to the north, and almost invisible in the darkness.

It was about half an hour later, perhaps even less, that that Spanish gunboat weighed her anchor and stole silently out to the open sea.

She breasted the fierce waves at the entrance to the inlet boldly. A minute later she was plowing her way through the storming sea. It was dark then and she could see nothing; but her captain had the course to a hair's breadth.

He knew which way his prey was gone, and he knew to what port she was going. He knew, too, that she would not dare go near the harbor of Key West until daylight. And so if by any chance he missed her in the darkness he would still have another opportunity.

And those on the shore who saw the vessel glide away chuckled gleefully to themselves. It was something to look forward to, a chance to revenge themselves upon the impudent Yankees who had dared to elude the fire from their guns.

Meanwhile the Yankees, totally unsuspicious of this last move, were buffeting their way bravely ahead.

The lookouts clinging to the railing in the bow were peering anxiously ahead in the darkness, and the sailors in the pilot house were wrestling with the wheel; it was quite a task to keep that vessel headed straight, for she was going into the very teeth of the gale.

And as for Clif, he was watchfulness personified. When he was not eyeing the compass carefully he was hurrying about the vessel, now down in the fire-rooms, making sure that those Spaniards were doing as they were ordered, and again looking the prisoners over to make sure that the sly rascals had not wriggled themselves free.

"It would be a fine thing to do," he thought to himself, "if they managed to recapture the ship."

There was something quite prophetic in that thought.

It is hard to keep awake all night, but a man can do it if he has to even though he has been working like a Trojan all day.

Clif kept moving to work off the sleepiness whenever he felt it coming on.

"I'll have time enough to sleep by and by," he muttered.

He was thinking, grimly enough, of how he would be stalled in the town of Key West with his prize, waiting for a chance to get out to the fleet again.

The vessel did not attempt to make more than half speed during the trip, and that, against the storm, was very little.

But there was no need to hurry thought every one.

And so for some two hours the vessel crept on, wearily as it seemed and monotonously. The only thing to vary matters was when some extra high wave would fling itself over the bow in a shower of spray.

But that was not a welcome incident, for it made it harder for the weary sailors to keep the course straight.

The cadet paced up and down the deck; he had been doing that for perhaps the last half hour, stopping only to say a cheery word to the lookouts and once to prop up Ignacio, who was being rolled unceremoniously about the deck.

The cunning Spaniard looked so bedraggled and miserable that Clif would have felt sorry for him if he had not known what a villain he was.

"He'd stab me again if he got a chance," he mused.

For Clif had saved that fellow's life once; but it had not made the least difference in his vindictive hatred.

"I'm afraid," Clif muttered, "that Ignacio will have to suffer this time."

The Spaniard must have heard him, for he muttered an oath under his breath.

"It would be wiser if it was a prayer," said the cadet. "Ignacio, you are near the end of your rope, and you may as well prepare for your fate."

The man fairly trembled all over with rage as he glared at his enemy; such rage as his was Clif was not used to, and he watched the man with a feeling of horror.

"I don't like Spaniards!" was the abrupt exclamation, with which he turned away.

And Ignacio gritted his teeth and simply glared at him, following back and forth his every move, as a cat might.

"I may have a chance yet," he hissed, under his breath. "Carramba, if I only had him by the throat!"

But Clif paid no more attention to the Spaniard. He had other things to attend to, things to keep him busy.

It was not very long before that was especially true. For some interesting events began to happen then.

They began so suddenly that there is almost no way to introduce them. The first signs of the storm was when it broke.

In the blackness of the night nothing could be seen, and the vessel was struggling along absolutely without suspicion. And Clif, as we have said, was walking up and down engrossed in his own thoughts, almost forgetting that he was out in the open sea where a Spanish warship might chance to be lurking.

And so it was literally and actually a thunderbolt from a clear sky.

The blackness of the waters was suddenly broken by a sharp flash of light, perhaps two hundred yards off to starboard.

And an instant later came the loud report of a gun.

The consternation of the Americans it would be hard to imagine. They were simply aghast, and Clif stood fairly rooted to the deck.

His mind was in a tumult, but he strove to think what that startling interruption could mean.

"They must have fired at us!" he gasped.

And if there was any doubt of that an instant later came a second flash.

To a merchantship in war time such a signal is peremptory. It means slow up or else take the consequences.

There were two possibilities that presented themselves to the commander of this particular merchantship. One was that he had met an American warship——

And the other! It was far less probable, but it was possible, and terrible. They might have fallen into the hands of the enemy.

But whatever was the case, there was nothing for Clif to do but obey the signals. He could not run and he could not fight.

"If I only knew," he thought, anxiously.

And then suddenly he learned; for a faint voice was borne over to him through the gale. It was a voice that spoke English!

"Ahoy there!" it rang.

And Clif roared back with all his might!

"Ahoy! What ship is that?"

And his heart gave a throb of joy when he heard:

"The United States cruiser Nashville. Who are you?"

"The Spanish merchantman Maria, in charge of a prize crew from the Uncas!"

Whether all that was heard in the roar of the storm Clif could not tell; but he put all the power of his lungs in it.

He knew that the story would be investigated.

And so he was quite prepared when he heard the response:

"Lay to and wait for a boarding party."

And quick as he could move Clif sprang to the pilot house, and signaled to stop, and the vessel swung round toward the stranger.

The die was cast, for good or evil. They had given up!

For perhaps five minutes there was an anxious silence upon the vessel. Every one was waiting anxiously, while the ship rolled in the trough of the sea and shook with the crashes of the waves. Her small crew were picturing in their minds what was taking place out there in the darkness, their comrades struggling to get a small boat out in that heavy sea.

And then they fancied them buffeting their way across, blinded by the spray and half swamped by the heavier waves.

"They can't be much longer," muttered Clif, impatiently.

"Ahoy there! A ladder!"

It seemed to come from right underneath the lee of the merchantman. And it was shouted in a loud, peremptory tone that was meant to be obeyed. A moment later the rope ladder was flung down. Clif peered over the side when he dropped it.

He could make out the shape of the boat tossing about below; he could even distinguish the figures of the men in the boat.

And then he made out a man climbing hastily up.

He stepped back to wait for him. He saw a blue uniform as the officer clambered up to the deck.

And then suddenly he stood erect, facing Clif.

The cadet took one glance at him and gave a gasp of horror.

It was a Spanish officer!

And he held in one hand a revolver and was aiming it straight at Clif's head.

CHAPTER VI.

REPELLING BOARDERS.

That had been a cleverly managed stroke, and it left the young officer simply paralyzed. All he could do was to stare into the muzzle of that weapon.

He realized of course in a flash how he had been duped. And he was in a trap!

Half dazed he looked and saw a Spanish sailor in the act of lifting himself up to the deck to join his superior. And Clif had no doubt there were half a dozen others following.

There was of course nothing that Clif could do; a movement on his part would have been sheer suicide.

He thought the case was hopeless; he had let himself be caught napping.

But the cadet had forgotten that there were other Americans on that vessel besides himself. And there were no revolvers threatening the others.

The rage of the Yankee tars at what seemed to them a cowardly and sneaking way to capture the ship was too great for them to control. Prudence would have directed surrender, for the Maria had not a gun on board and the Spaniard might blow her out of the water.

But nobody thought of that; the same instant the Spanish officer presented his weapon and disclosed his real nationality, there were two sharp cracks in instant succession from the bow of the imperiled ship.

And the officer staggered back with a gasp. He dropped his weapon to the deck, reeled for an instant and then vanished over the side in the darkness.

There was a moment of horror, and then Clif heard him strike with a thud on the small boat below.

At the same time there was a bright flash just in front of Clif, and a bullet whistled past his ear.

The Spanish sailor, who had only half reached the deck, had fired at him.

By that time there was no longer any hesitation as to what course to pursue. The sailors had decided it by their fatal shots. It was resistance to the death.

And Clif whipped out his own weapons and sent the sailor tumbling backward to follow his officer.

Then he drew his sword and with two slashing strokes severed the ladder. From the yells and confusion that followed there must have been quite a number clinging to the rope.

But where they were or what their fate was nobody had any time to learn. Everything was moving like lightning on the merchantman.

Clif leaped into the pilot house and signaled full speed. There was no further need of lookouts and so the two sailors rushed down into the engine-room to see that the order was obeyed.

The big vessel started slowly forward. The cadet sprang to the wheel, his mind in a wild tumult as he strove to think what he should do.

As if there were not confusion enough at that instant there were several loud reports in quick succession, followed by deafening crashes as shots tore through the vessel.

The Spaniards had opened fire!

"But they'll have to stop to pick up that boat's crew!" gasped Clif. "We may get away!"

And that being the case every minute was precious; the vessel had swung round, but there was no time to turn—she must run as she was for a while.

And from the way the vessel trembled and shook it could be told that the irate tars down below were making things hum.

"They may burst the boilers if they can," thought Clif, grimly.

The new course they were taking was south, exactly the opposite of the way they had been going. But Clif did not care about that.

"The storm will drive us faster!" he gasped. "And every yard counts."

The Spanish gunboat (nobody on the Maria, of course, knew but what she was a big cruiser) fired only about half a dozen shots at her daring enemy; then the yells of the crew of the small boat must have attracted her attention and forced her to desist for a moment.

"And now's our chance," was the thought of the Americans.

They were making the most of it, that was certain; they were fairly flying along with the great waves.

Clif himself was at the wheel, seeing that not an inch was lost by steering wrongly.

"We'll know soon," he muttered. "Very soon, for she'll chase us."

The scene at this time was intensely dramatic; for the big ship had glided out into the darkness and those on board of her could not see their pursuer. They had no means of telling where she was, or whether they had escaped or not.

They could only keep on listening anxiously, tremblingly, counting the seconds and waiting, almost holding their breath.

They knew what the signal would be. The signal of their failure. If the Spaniard succeeded in finding them, he would open fire and soon let them know.

Clif tried to guess how long it would take them to pick up the unfortunate occupants of that small boat.

"They'll be raging mad when they do," he thought. "Gorry! they'll murder every one of us."

For they would probably call the shooting of that officer a murder; it did not trouble Clif's conscience, for he knew that a merchant vessel has the same right to resist the enemy that a warship has. It was not as if they had surrendered and then imitated the example of the treacherous Ignacio.

"I wonder how Ignacio likes this anyhow," thought Clif.

But he had no time to inquire the Spaniard's views on the struggle; Clif was too busily waiting and counting the seconds.

He did not think it would be very long before the enemy's ship would be after them again; and yet several minutes passed before any sign of the pursuit was given.

Clif began to think that possibly they had eluded their would-be captors. But his hopes were dashed, for suddenly there came the dreaded warning shot.

And it was fired from so close that, though the Americans had been listening for it, it made them start. It was evident that the enemy's vessel had come close to do the business; her first shot seemed fairly to tear the big merchantman to pieces.

And Clif shut his teeth together with a snap.

"We're in for it now," he muttered. "That settles it."

There was no longer the last hope of escape. There was no longer even any use of keeping on. There were but two things to be considered, sink or surrender.

There was a grim smile on the cadet's face as he turned away from the wheel.

"Tell the two men to come up from below," he said to one of the sailors.

And then he went out on deck, staring in the direction of the pursuing vessel. There was no difficulty in telling where she was now, for a continuous flashing of her guns kept her in view.

Clif was cool, singularly cool, as he stood in his exposed position. He was no longer anxious, for he had no longer any hope. There was nothing on board the Maria that could cope with the enemy's guns. There was only the inevitable to be faced.

The cadet soon guessed the nature of the pursuer from the way she behaved. Her guns were all low down and close together. They were about three-pounders, and rapid-firing.

"It's a gunboat like the Uncas," he muttered. "Gorry! how I wish the Uncas would come back!"

But the Uncas was then near Havana, far from any possibility of giving aid. And Clif knew it, so he wasted no time in vain regrets.

By that time the Spanish vessel had gotten the range, and her three or four guns were blazing away furiously. The gunboat was alight with the flames of the quick reports, and the sound was continuous.

"They aren't doing as well as I did," Clif said. "But still, they'll manage to do the work."

And so it seemed, for shot after shot crashed through the hull of the already battered vessel. The Spaniards were mad, evidently. There was no hail this time and proposal to surrender. But only a calm setting to work to finish that reckless ship.

The sailors came on deck and Clif, when he saw them, turned and pointed to the Spaniard.

"There she is, men," he said. "Look her over."

For a moment nobody said anything; the little group stood motionless on the deck. They were in no great danger for the firing was all directed at the hull.

Then suddenly Clif began again.

"I guess this vessel is about done for," he said. "She will be either sunk or captured. The only question is about us—what's to become of us. I leave it to you."

None of the men spoke for a moment.

"I suppose," Clif said, "that we can manage to let her know we surrender if we choose. We can scuttle the ship before we do it. But you know what we may expect; after our shooting those two men they'll probably murder us, or do things that are a thousand times worse."

Clif stopped for a moment and then he turned.

"Think, for instance," he said, "of being at the mercy of that man."

He was pointing toward Ignacio, who lay near them, glowering in his hate, and the sailors looked and understood.

"It's better to drown, sir," said one.

And the rest thought so, too, and declared it promptly.

"Very well, then," was the cadet's quiet answer, "we will stay on board. We have faced death before."

That resolution made there was little else left to be determined.

"We can sink the ship, or wait and let them sink it," the cadet said. "Or else—there's one thing more. We are headed in the right direction. We can smash her upon the rocks of the Cuban coast."

And the sailors stared at him for a moment eagerly.

"And stand a chance of getting ashore in safety!" they cried.

At which the cadet smiled.

"I'm afraid there's very little chance," he said. "But it's as good as anything else. We'll try it."

"Yes, sir."

"You two go down to the engine room again, and keep things moving. And the others stay on deck and make sure those Spaniards don't try to board us again. I can handle the wheel myself."

And with that the brave cadet turned away and sprang toward the pilot house.

CHAPTER VII.

A DESPERATE CHASE.

That was a heroic resolution those five brave men had made. But it was inevitable, for they did not mean that either they or that valuable ship should fall into the hands of the enemy.

And apparently the enemy knew they did not mean to. For they kept battering away at the big hulk that loomed up in the darkness, running close alongside and firing viciously.

Every shot made a deafening crash as it struck home.

But the Americans did not mind it especially. When a man has made up his mind to die he is not afraid of anything.

And the men on deck paced up and down serenely, and Clif tugged at the wheel with a positively light-hearted recklessness.

It would have been a cold sort of a person whose spirit did not rise to such an occasion as that. The wild night and the furious cannonading, but above all the prospect of taking that huge ship and driving her forward at full speed until she smashed upon the rocks, was a rather inspiring one.

The reader may have heard about the man out West who drew an enormous crowd by advertising an exhibition railroad wreck, two empty trains crashing into each other at full speed. This was a similar case; it does not often happened that a man has occasion to drive a ship aground on purpose.

The resolution to which the Americans had come must have been plain to the unfortunate Spaniards who were tied up on board the Maria. Their fright was a terrible one, anyhow.

Clif glanced out at them several times; their presence was the only thing that made him hesitate to do what he had resolved.

"For they haven't done anything, poor devils," he thought to himself, "I wish I knew what to do with them."

But there was only one thing that could be done; that was to put them off in a small boat, and that would be practically murdering them.

"They'll have to stay and take chances with us," muttered Clif.

As if there were not noise enough about that time those men began to raise a terrific outcry, yelling and shrieking in terror. But nobody paid any attention to them—except that the sailors took the trouble to examine their bonds once more.

It would have been dangerous to let those desperate fellows get loose then. For the Americans had enemies enough to cope with as it was.

All this while the Spanish gunboat had been firing away with all her might and main. She would cut across the vessel's stern, and send her shots tearing through the whole length of the ship; then she would come up close alongside and pour a dozen broadsides in.

And nearly all the shots hit, too.

It was evident to those on board that the merchantman would not stand very much battering of that sort. Already one of the sailors had come up to announce that two of the firemen had been struck.

But still the Maria tore desperately onward. Nobody cared very much how much damage was done, except that they did not want the engines to be smashed until the ship had reached the shore.

As well as Clif could calculate roughly, it ought not to have taken them an hour to return to the coast, for they had the storm to aid them. That they could hold out that long under the unceasing fire he did not believe.

"But the Spaniards may use up all their ammunition," he thought to himself.

That was a possibility, for he knew that the supply in the possession of Spain was a small one.

And the actual course of events made him think that his surmise was true. The desperate chase kept up for perhaps half an hour; and then unaccountably the Spaniard's fire began to slacken.

Clif could hardly believe his ears when he heard it.

"What can it mean?" he gasped.

But a moment later his surprise was made still greater. For one of the sailors bounded into the pilot house.

"She's giving up, sir!" he cried.

"Giving up!"

"Yes, sir."

"How in the world do you mean?"

"She's stopped firing, sir. And what's more, she's dropping behind."

Clif stared at the man in amazement.

"Dropping behind!"

And then suddenly he sprang out to the deck.

"Take the wheel a moment," he cried to the sailor.

And he himself bounded down the deck toward the stern.

He stared out over the railing, clinging to it tightly to prevent himself from being flung off his feet.

He found that what the sailor had said was literally true. The Spaniard was now firing only an occasional shot, and she was at least a hundred yards behind.

What that could mean Clif had not the faintest idea. Could it be that her engines had met with an accident? Or that she fancied the merchantman was sinking?

The cadet gazed down into the surging water below him; he could see the white track of the big steamer and knew that she was fairly flying along.

He took one more glance in the direction of the now invisible Spaniard. The firing had ceased altogether.

And like a flash the thought occurred to Clif that whatever the reason for the strange act might be, now was the time to save the merchantman.

"We can turn off to one side!" he gasped, "and lose her!"

And with a bound he started for the pilot house.

"Hard a-port!" he shouted to the man at the wheel.

But before the man had a chance to obey Clif chanced to glance out ahead, into the darkness toward which the vessel was blindly rushing.

And the cadet staggered back with a gasp.

"A light!" he cried. "A light!"

Yes, there was a dim flickering point of light directly in front of them. Where it came from Clif could not tell, but he realized the significance in an instant.

And at the same time there was another sound that broke upon his ear and confirmed the guess. It was a dull, booming roar.

The man at the wheel heard it, too.

"It's breakers, sir!" he shouted. "Breakers ahead!"

They were nearing the land!

And then the significance of the Spaniard's act became only too apparent. The men who were running her had seen the light, and they had no idea of being led to destruction by their eagerness to follow that reckless merchantman.

And so they were slowing up and keeping off the shore.

There was a faint hope in that; the Maria might be able to steal away if she were quick enough in turning.

Clif's order had been obeyed by the sailor the instant he heard it. Clif sprang in to help him, and they whirled the wheel around with all their might.

But alas! they were too late! When a steamer waits until she hears breakers in a storm like that it is all up with her, for she must be near the shore indeed.

And plunging as the Maria was, urged on by wind and waves and her own powerful engines, it was but an instant before the crisis came.

Clif had half braced himself for the shock; but when it came it was far greater than he had expected. There was a crash that was simply deafening. The huge ship plunged into the rocky shore with a force that almost doubled her up, and made her shake from stem to stern. And she stopped so abruptly that Clif was flung through the window of the pilot house.

The deed was done!

CHAPTER VIII.

A DASH FOR THE SHORE.

Strange to say, Clif was not much excited at the terrific moment. The peril was so great that he was quite gay as he faced it. He had risen to the occasion.

He picked himself up and stepped out to the deck.

There he found a scene of confusion indescribable. Above the noise of the breakers on the shore and the waves that were flinging themselves against the exposed side of the ship rang the wild shrieks and cries of the terrified Spanish prisoners.

The vessel after she had struck had been flung around and was being turned farther over every minute. The violence of the storm that was struggling with her was quite inconceivable.

The waves were pouring over her in great masses, sweeping everything before them; and the spray was leaping so high and the flying storm clouds driving past so low that there was no telling where the surface of the sea ended and the air began.

The big ship had landed among rocks, and every wave was lifting her up and flinging her down upon them with dull, grinding crashes that could be both heard and felt.

A moment after she struck a man came dashing up the ladder to the deck; it was one of the sailors, and behind were the terrified firemen.

"She's leaking in a dozen places!" the man shouted.

He clung to railing as he spoke, and a great wave half drowned him; but he managed to salute, and Clif saw a look of wild delight on his face, one that just corresponded with his own eager mood.

"She'll split in about half a minute, I fancy," the cadet answered, "and the Spaniards are welcome to what's left. We've done our duty."

And with that he turned to the pilot house, where the rest of the men were grouped. They were gazing at him eagerly.

"Are you ready, boys?" Clif shouted.

Every one knew what he meant by "ready"—ready to make the wild attempt to land and reach the shore through all those wildly surging breakers. The very thought of it was enough to stir one's blood.

And the answer came with a vengeance.

"Ay, ay, sir!"

"Then get out one of the boats," shouted Clif.

As he saw the men struggling forward to reach the nearest rowboat he turned suddenly on his heel. He had something else to attend to for a moment.

It was an errand of mercy. Those shrieking wretches were all bound to the railing of the doomed ship, and Clif would never have forgiven himself if he had left them there. Their faces would have haunted him.

And he drew his sword and set swiftly to work.

He cut the captain loose and put a knife into his hand.

"Get to work!" he cried. "Get to work!"

Clif took the risk of trusting the man, and went on, leaving him with the weapon. The cadet believed that he would be grateful for his release.

And besides they were fellow sufferers then, threatened with the same peril.

And Clif was not mistaken. The man set hastily to work releasing his comrades, and in less time than it takes to tell it the terrified men were huddled together on the deck.

The cadet wasted no more time upon them.

"There are three boats left for you," he cried. "Save yourselves."

And with that he turned and made his way down to where his own men were struggling with one of the small boats.

There was one other thing which in the wild confusion of that moment Clif managed to remember needed to be attended to. There was Ignacio!

The treacherous Spaniard had nearly been swept off, and he was half drowned by the floods of water that poured over the deck. But his hatred of the Americans was too great for him to shout to them for aid.

What to do with that murderous villain was a problem that worried Clif. Undoubtedly the wisest thing would be to kill him, then and there; death was the fate he certainly deserved.

And Clif half drew his sword; but it was no use. He could not bring himself to do such an act. And he flung the weapon back into the scabbard.

To attempt to carry him away was equally useless; the Americans did not expect to reach the shore themselves.

"I'll leave him to his fate," Clif muttered. "The Spaniards may help him if they choose."

And with that he turned toward the sailors again; the men had by that time nearly succeeded in getting the boat away. They were working like Trojans.

Every wave that struck the ship helped to fill the boat, even before it touched the water; the spray poured down over the slanting deck upon it and the sailors had to empty it several times.

While they were wrestling thus the wind and water and rocks had been getting in their work upon the doomed vessel. Lower and lower she sank, harder and harder she pounded.

And then suddenly a great billow heaved itself with a thud against the bow and fairly hammered it around. One of the sailors gave a yell.

"She's split!"

And sure enough, a great seam had opened amidships and the water surged in with a roar.

The vessel seemed fairly falling to pieces.

And such being the case the sailors had no time to delay. The frail boat was lowered into the seething waters; the men tumbled in and seized the oars. Clif made a wild leap and caught the stern just as one mighty wave raced by and whirled the boat away from the vessel.

And in one instant it was lost to sight and sound. What was done by the Spaniards no one could see a thing. The Americans were fighting for their own lives.

There was but one thing for them to do——

"Pull for the shore, sailors, pull for the shore."

And the great sweeping breakers to aid them. In fact they were flung in so fast that they could hardly row.

It was a thrilling struggle, that race with the giant waves. The sailors struggled with all their might, keeping the frail craft straight. And Clif, with a bucket he had thought to bring, was bailing frantically, and shouting to encourage the men.

In, in they swept, nearer, with the speed of a whirlwind, toward the shore.

"If it's rocks, Heaven help us!" Clif gasped.

It seemed an age to him, that brief struggle. Breathless and eager, he watched the great white caps breaking, smiting against the stern, struggling to turn that boat but a few inches so that they might catch it on the side and fling it over.

And meanwhile the wind and waves and oars all helping, on swept the boat—bounding over the foamy crests, sinking into the great hollows, leaping and straining, but still shooting on in the darkness.

And every second was precious, for the shore was not far away; the roar of the surf grew louder—louder almost upon them.

And then suddenly one great seething billow came rushing up behind. Clif saw it, and shouted to the men. In a second more its white crest towered over them.

It was just on the point of breaking in a giant cataract of foam; it would have buried the little boat and its occupants beneath tons of foaming water.

But it was just a second too late. The little boat's stern shot up; for a moment it was almost on end, and then it rose to the top of the wave and a moment later as the crash came and the sweep in toward shore began the frail craft was flung forward as if from a catapult.

And in it shot with speed that simply dazed the Americans; but it was toward shore—toward shore!

They had passed the breakers!

And Clif gave a gasp of delight as he felt the wild leap forward. It seemed but a second more before the rush ended.

The bow of the rowboat struck and the frail object was whirled round and flung over, its occupants being fairly hurled into the air.

When they struck the water it was to find themselves within a few feet of dry land. They staggered to a standing position to find that they were in water only up to their waists. And the great wave was tugging them out to sea again.

They struggled forward wildly, clutching at each other. A minute later, breathless, exhausted and half drowned, but wild with joy, they staggered out upon a sandy beach and sank down to gasp for breath.

"We're safe!" panted Clif. "Safe!"

Safe! And on the island of Cuba, the stronghold of their deadly enemies!

CHAPTER IX.

THE ENEMY'S COUNTRY.

It must have been at least five minutes before those exhausted men moved again; when at last they managed to rise to their feet it was to find themselves in the midst of absolute darkness, with the wild sea on one side of them and on the other no one knew what.

The faint point of light which they had seen had now disappeared: but they took it to mean that there were Spaniards in the neighborhood.

And they did not fail to recognize the peril in which they were. The firing had probably been heard and the wreck of the merchantman seen. If so, the Americans could not be in a much worse place.

"We may be right in front of a battery," whispered Clif.

The first thing the sailors did was to see to their revolvers and cutlasses. And after that they started silently down the shore.

"We won't try to go far," Clif said, "but we must find a hiding-place."

But in that darkness the hiding-places were themselves hidden; the best the Americans could do was to stumble down the shore for a hundred yards or so, being careful to walk where the waves would wash out their footprints.

Then they were a short distance from the wreck and felt a trifle safer.

"We may as well strike back in the country now," said the leader, "at least until we can find some bushes or something to conceal us."

That was a rather more ticklish task, and the men crouched and stole along in silence. They had no idea what they might meet.

It was fortunate for them that they were quiet. Otherwise they would have gotten into very serious trouble indeed.

They stole up the sandy beach a short ways, feeling their way along and getting further and further away from the sea. They were struggling through soft dry sand.

And suddenly Clif, who was in front, saw something loom up before him, a dark line. And he put out his hand to touch it.

He found that the sand rose gradually into a sort of drift or bank. It was high, and seemed to reach for some distance.

The sailors stopped abruptly, and Clif crept softly forward, feeling along with his hands; suddenly the men heard him mutter a startled exclamation under his breath.

"Men," he whispered, "we're in a terrible fix; I ran into a gun!"

"A gun!"

"Yes—a big one. We've struck a Spanish battery, and we must be near some town!"

The sailors stared at him aghast; and then suddenly came a startling interruption—one that fairly made their blood grow chill.

"Who goes there?"

It was a loud, stern hail in Spanish, and it seemed to come from almost beside them!

Quick as a flash the Americans dropped, crouching close together in the darkness. They could hear the beating of each others' hearts.

There were several moments of agonizing suspense; the Spaniard who had shouted out was evidently awaiting a reply. And then suddenly he repeated his challenge.

"Who goes there?"

And a moment later came a sound of hurrying footsteps.

"What's the matter?" Clif heard a voice demand.

He was the only one in the party who understood Spanish, and knew what was said. But it was plain to the rest that it was a conversation between a sentry and an officer.

"I heard a footstep, senor capitan!" cried the man. "Quidada! Take care! It's very near."

There was a moment's pause.

"You must be mistaken," said the officer.

"I am not mistaken," repeated the man firmly. "Santa Maria, my ears do not deceive me. You said to be watchful, for you have heard firing."

To that the Americans had listened in trembling silence; but the next made them jump. "I will light this lantern," said the officer.

And the instant they heard it Clif rose silently to his feet; the men did likewise, and began to creep softly off to one side.

But careful as they were they could not help the grinding sound of their footsteps in the sand, and it caught the quick ear of the Spaniard.

"Hear it!" he cried. "Por dios, again! Somebody is stealing upon us!"

And an instant later the air was rent by a sharp crack of a rifle—the sentry had fired!

There was wild confusion at once, and the unfortunate castaways were aghast. For an instant Clif thought of charging the battery—with four men. But he realized the folly of that.

"Quick!" he cried, "let us hide. Forward!"

Lights were flashing and men shouting and running about behind the sand wall just in front of them, but the sailors were still unseen. They broke into a run and fairly flew down the shore.

They fancied the whole Spanish company was at their heels; but after they had run for some distance they found that they had not been pursued.

For the enemy were so taken by surprise at the sudden alarm that they were if possible more frightened than the Americans.

And so the men stopped for breath.

They stared at each other, as if hardly able to realize the peril into which they had so suddenly been plunged.

"I think that was the quickest adventure I ever had in my life," muttered Clif.

The suddenness of it made him laugh; they had almost walked into a Spanish fort.

But it was no laughing matter, certainly; it was a confounded piece of ill-luck.

"For they'll be watching for us now!" muttered Clif. "I'm afraid that will settle us."

"They'll follow our footsteps!" exclaimed one of the sailors.

That was so, and it was an unpleasant prospect; it was plain that if the Americans wished to find any safety they must get some distance away from that battery.

"We'll make one more effort to get back into the country," muttered Clif.

And amid silence and anxious suspense they once more started up the sloping seashore.

They crept along as it seemed by inches. But fortunately they did not run across any more "guns." When they came across an embankment it was of solid earth and marked the end of the beach.

And there were some trees and bushes there, so the Americans began to feel more comfortable. For all they knew they might in the darkness have been strolling into a town.

But they were apparently out in the open country, there seemed to be no people and no houses near. So they started boldly forward.

It was then late at night, a dark and damp and windy night; so they were not likely to find many people wandering about.

"What we want to do," Clif said, "is to get back in the country a while where we can hide until morning. Then if we can find some Cubans we'll be all right."

Clif was about tired to death. He had done far more work that day than any of those sailors. But there was no time for resting then.

He gritted his teeth and started; they took their bearings from the sea, and then went straight on, watching and listening carefully, but meeting with no trouble.

At first their walk led through what had evidently once been a cultivated country, for it was level and had but few trees upon it. At present, however, it was overgrown with weeds.

Once they almost ran into a house, which it may readily be believed gave them a start. It was creepy business, anyhow, this stumbling along through the enemy's country without being able to see ten yards in front.

But the house seemed to be empty. In fact, it could hardly be called a house any more, for it was half burned down.

The Americans thought that it was empty, for Clif had stumbled and fallen with a crash over a pile of dry sticks and rubbish. But when he rose to his feet to listen anxiously there was no movement or sign that anybody had heard him.

"It probably belonged to some of the reconcentrados," he muttered.

He was about to turn and give the word to proceed.

Then suddenly a new idea occurred to him, and he gave a pleased exclamation.

"This is lucky!" he whispered. "Men, what is the matter with hiding there?"

That was a rather startling proposition; for they could not be at all sure but some one lived there after all.

But Clif had come several miles by that time, and he was disposed to be a trifle desperate.

A person can get so tired that he will be anxious to enter even a Spanish dungeon in order to get a chance to rest.

"We will search the house," he said. "If we find anybody we'll hold them up and make them prisoners; and if we don't, we'll spend the night there."

And then without another word he started silently forward. The sailors were right behind him.

What was evidently the front of the house was the part that had been burned. Clif picked his way over the ruins and into the rear, where there was a roof still remaining.

There was a door there, half shut; one may readily believe that in pushing it open Clif was rather nervous.

But nothing occurred to startle him, and so they went forward once more. The place about him seemed deserted.

Then suddenly Clif did a startling thing.

He took a deep breath and called aloud.

"Anybody here?"

And then for at least a minute or two the little party stood waiting in silence; but no answer was heard.

"I guess it's deserted," Clif said. "Scatter and search it thoroughly."

And that was quickly done. To their relief the Americans found that the place was not inhabited and that there was no one near. That once made sure it may be believed that they wasted no more time in delay.

"I don't think it will be necessary for us to keep watch," he said. "Our safety lies in our hiding."

They made their way into one of the smaller rooms of the little building, one which had a key to the door. And having secured themselves as best they could from danger of discovery, the wearied men sank down upon the floor.

CHAPTER X.

A STARTLING DISCOVERY.

It may seem strange that they were able to sleep in the perilous situation they were in; but they were men who were used to holding their lives in their hands. They say that Napoleon could take a nap, during a lull in battle, while he was waiting for his reserves to be brought up.

The men were cold and damp, of course, but it was impossible for them to light a fire, even had they dared to take such a risk. But the darkness was their principal shield.

But all the cold in the world could not have kept Clif awake; he and the rest of the men were soon fast asleep, hidden away in the enemy's country, and surrounded by perils innumerable, yet resting as quietly as if they were at home.

And none of them awakened either, as the dark night wore on. The day began to break over the mountains to the eastward, and the gay sunbeams streamed into the room to find the sailors still undisturbed and unconscious.

The sun had risen and was half an hour up in the sky before any of the Americans showed signs of awakening. One of the sailors turned over and then sat up and stared about him.

It was not strange that the man wondered where he was, for a moment; he had been through so much during the previous day.

He found himself seated in a little bare apare apartment half charred by fire, and having damp straw for flooring. His companions, including the officer, were stretched out upon it.

They seemed in blissful ignorance of the fact that it was damp.

The sailor rose to his feet; he was rather stiff and sore, and somewhat hungry, but he felt that he ought to be glad to be alive.

And then he stole quickly over to the tiny window to look out; naturally enough he was a little curious to see what sort of a place it was they had hit on in the darkness.

There was light, then, plenty of it—too much in fact, so the man thought. It showed him everything.

And the everything must have included something rather startling. For the sailor acted in a most surprising way.

He took a single glance out of the window; and then he staggered back as if some one had shot him.

The man's face was as white as a sheet.

He stood for a moment seemingly dazed, his eyes staring vacantly. And then suddenly he made a leap across the room and seized Clif by the shoulder.

It was a startling way for Clif to be awakened; the face of that man had a sort of nightmare look.

"What is it?" Clif gasped. "Quick!"

"The window!" panted the sailor. "Look!".

The man in his excitement had awakened the rest and they were sitting up staring at him.

Clif meanwhile had rushed to the window, and when he looked out he acted just as the sailor had done.

It might be well to describe in a few words what he saw.

There was a small clearing around the deserted building, and beyond that a heavy wood. Clif remembered having made his way through those woods.

And now somebody else had done likewise. There was a squad of a dozen soldiers standing on the clearing's edge.

And they were Spaniards!

"Can they have surrounded us?" gasped the cadet.

"Or perhaps they don't know we're here," whispered one of the men.

The full meaning of that startling discovery was made evident to them an instant later. The officer of the Spaniards was standing to one side watching a man, who, with bowed head, was carefully scanning the ground.

And he was coming slowly toward the building.

"They're tracking us," whispered Clif.

And just then the man raised up his head and Clif got a glimpse of his face.

"The villain!" he gasped.

It was Ignacio!

Yes, it was the villainous Spanish spy. He and his Spanish companions must have succeeded in getting ashore. And they had tracked their unsuspecting enemies to their hiding-place.

"I wish I had killed him!" Clif muttered half to himself.

One of the sailors heard him, and he drew his revolver significantly.

"It's not too late, sir," he said.

But Clif held up his hand.

"No, no," he whispered. "Not yet!"

That suggestion called him back to action. Not yet—because they had not yet been discovered.

Ignacio was apparently off the scent; he did not know whether his victims had dodged the building or had the temerity to enter.

And instantly Clif leaped forward, over to the other side of the building. If none of the enemy was there it might not be too late for flight.

"If they are," Clif muttered to himself, "by jingo, they've still got the building to capture."

Whatever was to be done had to be done quickly, for Ignacio was a cunning fellow, and wouldn't be apt to delay very long.

Clif gazed out in the other direction and saw to his delight that the thicket came close to the house, and there were no Spaniards in sight.

He called in a low voice to the men, who stole silently over toward him.

"Quick!" he gasped. "Out, for your lives!"

It was a thrilling moment, and Clif was trembling with eagerness. One by one he watched the men crawl out of the low window and gather in the shelter of the building.

And a moment later he himself dropped down; the instant he struck the ground he started forward.

"To the woods!" he whispered. "And not a sound, for your lives."

And the men sprang softly forward, not even pausing to glance over their shoulders to see if they were discovered.

Clif fancied at that instant that he was safe. The building was between him and the Spaniards.

But he did not know that at that moment Ignacio had observed a footprint in the damp ground that made him aware that they had gone into the building; he rushed around to the other side just in time to see a blue uniform vanish in the thicket.

The next moment a wild yell came from his throat.

"Mira!" he shrieked. "Forward! Here they are now!"

CHAPTER XI.

A RUNNING FIGHT.

That cry seemed the death knell of the Americans, and their hearts leaped up in their throats when they heard it. For a moment Clif thought of stopping and giving battle then and there.

But he realized the hopelessness of that; it was hopeless too, to run, with no place to run to. But the sailors were already dashing away through the woods. And the cadet soon caught up with them and urged them on.

The Spaniards broke into a run the moment they heard Ignacio's cry; a minute later they fired a volley into the bushes, probably in order to alarm the country.

It would have been hard for those five fugitives to go any faster than they did during the first few moments of that chase. They heard their enemies banging away and yelling in their rear, and they fairly flew over the ground.

"Keep together," panted Clif. "We may find some place to make a stand."

The ground over which they were traveling was ill adapted for speed, for it was rough and the bushes were thick.

But it was as fair for one as the other, and the Americans tore their way through and sped on.

The Spaniards in the rear apparently knew of other troops in the neighborhood from the way they kept yelling; Clif groaned as he realized the hopelessness of their flight.

For even if they succeeded in shaking off their pursuers the whole country was alarmed and hunting for them. And they had no food and no one to guide them.

But the present evil was great enough, for the furious Spaniards were hot on the trail.

"Surrender! Surrender!" Clif heard the officer shouting a short way back.

The chase would have ended in no time had it not been for the woods, which kept the fugitives out of sight so that they could not be shot.

But that was a protection that would not last forever. Clif gave a sudden gasp as he saw a clearing ahead of them.

But it was only a small one, and the Americans sped across it at the very top of their speed. They hoped to reach the woods before their foes sighted them.

And they did. Then suddenly a new idea flashed over Clif.

"Stop a minute!" he cried. "Ready!"

The sailors saw him draw his revolver, and they knew what it meant. They crouched in the bushes, waiting.

"We'll show them it isn't all play," Clif whispered.

And, a second later, half a dozen Spaniards dashed out of the woods.

"Fire!" roared Clif.

There was a quick volley, and then instantly the fugitives sprang up again and sped on. They left several of their enemies lying on the ground.

That unexpected move had evidently disconcerted the pursuers, who hadn't looked for a reception of that kind.

They were not heard on the trail again for fully a minute, while the Americans made the best possible use of their time. But the pursuers did not mean to give up as easily as that, and they soon set out once more, firing away as if a whole army were in sight.

Their little success raised the spirits of the gallant tars considerably; they seemed to forget they were in the enemy's country.

And they chuckled gleefully to themselves as they raced on through the woods; they were a pretty small army of invasion, but they had lots of courage.

But there is a limit to what courage can do, and the unfortunate sailors soon learned it.

They came to a second clearing, a broad savanna this time.

"We'll have to run for our very lives," gasped Clif.

For if they failed to reach shelter before the Spaniards came up the former situation would be just reversed and the Spaniards could hide and fire in safety.

And so the men set out at breakneck speed, as if they were in a hundred yard's dash.

"I think we can make it," thought Clif. "They seem to be a long ways behind."

The shouts of the enemy indicated it; Clif's volley had seemed to deprive them of their former confidence and rashness.

But unfortunately, they were not the only Spaniards in Cuba. The firing had not failed to attract attention.

The Americans had reached about the centre of the broad plain. There was high grass and cane upon it, and that made even walking hard. But the men still plunged on bravely, though they were gasping for breath.

But then something happened that made them gasp still more.

For the shouts of the enemy in the rear were suddenly answered.

And the answer came from in front.

The sailors halted and stared at each other in consternation.

"Do you see anything?" cried Clif.

All that could be made out was a line of bushes and undergrowth, marking the beginning of the woods.

But out of it came a confused babel of shouts, as if a whole army were there and had been suddenly alarmed.

"They'll head us off!" gasped the sailor.

But they stood still for only a second; now was no time to delay.

The pursuers in the rear were drawing closer every instant.

There was only one thing left. They were shut off in two directions, but off to each side——

"Come!" gasped Clif.

And the sailors whirled about and followed him in the new direction. It was a hopeless hope, but it was not yet time to give up.

And so for perhaps a hundred yards they raced on. They had heard a shout behind them, and saw the Spaniards running out from the woods, both in front and behind.

"Turn and fight them!" shouted Clif.

Like wild animals at bay the sailors faced about and jerked out their revolvers again. They were on the point of opening fire, when suddenly, as if they were not in trouble enough, there came a new development.

There was a yell behind them, and a crashing sound. Out upon the broad savanna galloped a whole troop of Spanish cavalry, their carbines in their hands.

And at their head rode a brightly uniformed captain waving his sword and galloping down upon the fugitives.

"Surrender!" he yelled. "Lay down your arms."

And that was the last straw; the sailors looked at Clif, and Clif looked at the sailors. The troopers were not a hundred yards away, and there were fifty of them.

"I guess we may as well give up," said Clif, grimly. "We've done our best, I think."

And he turned toward the galloping men, dropped his sword and revolver, and then folded his arms.

"We surrender," he called. "Come on."

And a minute later the gallant five were surrounded by the cavalrymen, who stared at them eagerly.

"Who are you?" demanded the gruff captain.

"An officer in the United States Navy," said Clif, promptly. "From the gunboat Uncas."

"And what are you doing here?"

"We were wrecked on the coast last night. We surrender, and we expect to be decently treated."

"You are prisoners of war," was the officer's stern response, "and you will be treated as such. Forward, march!"

CHAPTER XII.

THE FIRST PRISONERS OF WAR.

The command had hardly been obeyed when out from the brush at the further side of the savanna came the pursuing Spaniards and with them Ignacio.

The latter made straight for Clif with an upraised dagger, and would have killed the cadet then and there if the commander of the troop had not prevented him forcibly.

"You fool!" he said, "don't you know the orders?"

"What orders?"

"From Blanco. Prisoners are to be brought to Havana. If you want to kill him, wait till you get him there."

And so the furious Ignacio was compelled to leave his enemy alone. He now rode along behind the troopers, muttering curses under his breath.

But he knew that his time would come later; moreover he had not so very long to wait, for the capture had been made quite near to Havana.

The country through which they were riding was broad and flat, rising gradually to the blue hills at the southward. All about them it seemed as if the land had once been under cultivation; but now it was overgrown with rank vegetation.

In the distance could be seen the buildings of a little town, for which they were heading.

The Spanish cavalrymen rode along merrily, their accoutrements jingling. They were a dark-skinned, black-haired lot, and most of them were small, and not very sturdily built. The Americans had heard it said that they didn't get enough to eat, and they looked it.

The prisoners were mounted upon spare horses, and were kept well in the middle of the group. Their hands were tied behind them, and one of their captors had hold of the bridles of their mounts.

Clif's was a jaded old nag, and kept stumbling and stopping, making the task of riding a difficult one, but he did not notice it very much, for he was busily thinking.

His present situation was indeed a discouraging one, and he felt its degradation keenly. It was not that his conscience troubled him, for he knew that he had done all that could be expected of him.

But he was a prisoner for all that, and he had before him all the horrors of which he had heard so much.

Still there was no chance of escape, and he could only bow to the inevitable; but he could not help feeling a thrill of apprehension as he glanced behind him and saw the malignant Ignacio gazing at him.

But Ignacio bided his time, and said nothing. Meanwhile, the troopers trotted on.

In about fifteen minutes the little town drew near. Clif did not know the name of it, for he had no idea where he had run ashore on the previous night. But he did not think he was far from Havana.

The arrival of the soldiers created intense excitement in the town. Men and women and children and barking dogs rushed out to see them pass.

And when it was discovered that five Yankees had been captured the cavalrymen received an ovation. But they made straight on to their destination; what it was Clif had no trouble in guessing.

There was a railroad station in the town, and there the troopers came to a halt. Most of them dismounted from their horses to rest, and the captain hurried off to attend to the task of getting a train to take those prisoners to the capital.

Meanwhile a great crowd gathered about the little station; most of them were ugly-looking, ragged men, and they crowded around the prisoners and stared at them curiously.

There were looks of hatred upon their unpleasant faces, and their remarks it may be believed were not complimentary.

"The Yankee pigs have met their match at last," snarled one tobacco-stained peon, who had forced his way up close to Clif.

"And they'll go to Havana as they wanted to," put in another, with a leer. "They were boasting they'd get there."

There were some grins at that sally, which encouraged the Spaniard to go on.

"How do you like it?" he inquired. "Santa Maria, couldn't you have run fast enough?"

"They won't run any more," snarled another. "They'll be put where they're safe."

An old woman with a haggard, savage-looking face and a heavy stick shook the latter in the Americans' faces, as she cursed them in her shrill, Spanish jargon.

And then suddenly came a loud cry from the outskirts of the crowd.

"Stone the pigs! Kill 'em! Don't let them get away!"

Clif could not see the man who yelled that, but he knew the voice, and realized that Ignacio was getting in his fine work again.

And he seemed likely to be successful, too, for the cry appeared to please the crowd.

"Yes, yes, kill 'em!" swelled the muttering shout.

And a moment later some one, perhaps Ignacio himself, flung a heavy stone at the Americans.

It sailed over the heads of the mob, and struck one of the sailors a glancing blow on the forehead.

It made an ugly wound, and blood flowed.

The sight seemed to please the crowd.

"Por dios!" they laughed. "Good for them! Keep it up!"

Perhaps the sight of blood enraged them; but at any rate, their hostility became more evident. They shook their fists and muttered savagely.

And all the while Ignacio's voice chimed in.

"Kill 'em! Kill 'em!"

The prisoners seemed about to have a very unpleasant experience indeed. There was no one to restrain the crowd except the soldiers and they sympathized with the angry people.

And the crowd seemed to know that; they surged nearer.

"A prison's too good for them!" they roared.

The old hag was still shaking her cane and yelling her maledictions. At that moment a man snatched the stick from her hand and aimed a blow at Clif's face.

The cadet's hands were tied behind him, and he was nearly helpless. But he managed to turn and catch the blow upon his shoulders.

And an instant later his foot shot out and caught the enraged Spaniard squarely in the stomach.

The man staggered back.

"Madre di dios!" he gasped. "He's killed me."

Clif's daring action set the crowd in a perfect frenzy.

"Stone 'em!" yelled Ignacio.

And seemingly all at once they sprang at the prisoners with sticks and stones and knives and fists.

The soldiers made a feeble effort to stop them, but the crowd saw them laughing as they did so.

"Nobody cares about the Yankee pigs!" the crowd roared. "Go for them."

It would have gone hard with the Americans just then had it not been for the fact that the captain reappeared. He had no love to waste on them, but he knew his duty.

And he sprang forward with a stern command:

"Drive that crowd back! Quick!"

And then the cavalrymen acted in a quite different manner. The angry mob was forced away, in spite of their protests. The sailors breathed somewhat more freely.

Still it was to their relief when they saw an engine and a single freight car coming up the track. They knew that was for them and that they would soon be out of the reach of that mob.

"But not of Ignacio!" Clif groaned. "Not of Ignacio."

The "private car" intended for the strangers came to a stop in front of the little station, and they were told to dismount from the horses and enter.

The crowd gave a parting jeer as they lost sight of them. Once inside the sailors were gruffly ordered to sit down, and their feet were tied securely.

A sergeant and three men were detailed to mount guard over them, and then everything was ready for the start.

Clif watched anxiously for one thing; he had an idea that his deadly enemy might not succeed in following them the rest of the journey.

But in that he soon saw that he was mistaken. Ignacio had no idea of being foiled in his vengeance. Just before the door of the car was shut his small, crouching figure entered.

He stopped just long enough to clinch his fist and shake it at Clif; and then he retired into a corner to snarl angrily to himself.

A few moments later there was a creaking of wheels and the "train" had started. The roar of the crowd died away and was succeeded by the sound of the rapid motion.

The prisoners were on their way to Havana.

"And I wish there'd be a wreck and end us before we got there," mused Clif.

CHAPTER XIII.

IGNACIO'S PLOTS.

For Clif Faraday had not failed to learn something of what a prisoner might expect in Havana. A classmate of his, Vic Rollins, had spent a couple of months there and had emerged almost a physical wreck.

And Clif could not tell how long he might have to remain. The war had already been going on long enough for him to see that it would last some time.

And the amount of cruelty and starvation he had before him was enough to make the cadet tremble.

He knew that the severest privation would fall to his lot.

Ignacio could be trusted to see to that.

"I don't think they'll dare to let him kill me," the American muttered. "But he'll probably get his satisfaction somehow."

At any rate, it was plain that the vengeful Spaniard meant to try. He soon set to work.

That Clif understood Spanish he was well aware. But he did not seem to mind it.

For he began a conversation with the sergeant. And he did not take the trouble to whisper what he had to say, though one would have thought he would not care to have so villainous a plot known to any one.

The officer in charge of the Americans was sitting near them with his own sword lying in his lap. And Ignacio crept over to him.

"Jose," said he, "Jose Garcia, listen to me."

"What is it?"

"Jose, have you been paid your wages for the last six months?"

The soldier gazed at Ignacio in astonishment.

"Carramba! What's that to you?"

"Nothing, Jose, except that you need money, don't you?"

It was evident from the look that came over the Spanish soldier's face that the answer he made was sincere.

"Santa Maria!" he cried. "Yes! Why?"

"Would you like to make some?"

"How much?"

Slowly Ignacio reached his hand inside of his shirt and pulled out a little bag.

He loosened the mouth of it and took the contents out. He spread them out on the floor of the car.

"It is American money," he said, "the money of the pigs. But it is good money for all that."

"How much is there?"

"Ha! ha! You are interested, are you? Well, well!"

Ignacio's dark eyes glittered as he slowly went over the pile of bills.

"See, sergeant," said he, "here is a hundred-dollar bill. Just think of it! Look at it! Think if I should get that bill changed into good Spanish gold. The British consul would do it."

"Yes, he is a friend of the Yankees."

"Yes, he would do it for me. And then here is fifty dollars more. Look and count it. Think of what you could do with one hundred and fifty dollars of the Yankee's money. Think of what it would buy—food and I know not what—a fine dress for your sweetheart, to take her away from that rival of yours. And it is all good money, too."

"How am I to know it?"

"Carramba! Couldn't you take my word. You know me, Jose, and what I do for Spain. Do you not know that I am a friend of Blanco's? Hey? And you know that he trusts me when he trusts nobody else."

"And how did you get that money?"

"How did I get it! Ha! ha! I will tell—yes, por dios, I will, and those Yankee pigs may hear me, too. Ha! ha! There was what they called a traitor on the New York, the Yankee's flagship. She isn't much, but she is the best they have. One of our little gunboats could whip her, for it would be men fighting pigs."

The sergeant's eyes danced.

"And we'll sink her, too," went on Ignacio. "Just wait! I saw her run away once from a little gunboat. The Yankees build their boats swifter than ours so they can run away. But anyhow, as I said this man was working for Spain. And he tried to blow up the flagship."

"Por dios!" cried the sergeant, "like we did the Maine."

"Exactly. It would have been another glorious triumph for us. And, Jose Garcia, who do you think it was that prevented him?"

The man clinched his fists.

"I don't know!" he cried, "but I wish I could get hold of him."

"You do?"

"Yes."

"What would you do to him?"

"Santa Maria! I'd get him by the throat——"

"You would?"

"Yes. And I would choke him till he was dead."

"Dead!" echoed Ignacio, with a hoarse cry of triumph.

And then he raised one arm trembling all over with rage and hatred.

"Jose!" he half yelled.

"What is it?"

"Suppose I should tell you, Jose—suppose I should tell you that the villain is here?"

"Here?"

"Yes. By Heaven, he's here. Jose, that is he!"

And the fellow pointed straight at Clif, while he leaned forward and stared into the Spaniard's face, eager to see what the effect of his announcement would be.

It must have suited him, for he gave a low laugh, a fiendish chuckle.

Then he went on.

"And not only that, Jose! Think of what else he has done."

"Has he done more?"

"Yes, por dios, he has. Listen. Jose, we have in our power the worst of our country's enemies. Jose, he is a fiend, a perfect devil. He has ruined nearly every plan I tried. Do you know if it had not been for him—yes, for him— I should have stabbed the great pig admiral."

"Carramba!"

"Yes."

"Not Sampson."

"Yes, he, the villain who is blockading Havana and destroying our ships. I had the knife at his heart, and that Yankee pig prevented me. Do you wonder that I hate him?"

"No. I hate him, too."

"Yes! For you are a true Spaniard. But about that money, Jose. I got it as I say, from this Schwartz. For when this Yankee pig stopped him from blowing up the New York he ran away and hid. And he paid me this for helping him to Cuba."

Ignacio held up the bills before the hungry eyes of the Spanish sergeant.

And when he had given him time to look at it and think of what it meant for him, Ignacio suddenly bent forward and got close to him.

"Jose," he cried, "it's all for you!"

The man stared eagerly.

"What for?" he cried.

"I will tell you!" said Ignacio.

Once more he slipped his hand under his jacket.

"Look," said he.

And he drew out a sharp, gleaming dagger!

He ran his fingers over the edge, hissing as he did so between his teeth.

"It is sharp," he muttered. "Ha! ha! sharp! And it will do the work."

"What work?"

"Listen, Jose. There lies the fiend of a Yankee. He is in my power at last. He has baffled me, ruined me, but now I have him! Yes, he can't get away! Ha! ha! I feel merry. Jose, he is my deadliest enemy; he is your enemy, too, the enemy of our glorious country. I hate him—so must you."

"I do!"

"Then listen. I want to take this knife, this nice, sharp knife that I have been grinding for him. Ha! ha! Santa Maria, how sharp it is! And I will put this money, all this money, into your hands and you will turn away so as not to see. And I will take this knife in my hand so. And I will creep over toward that fellow——"

"And kill him?"

"Listen, Jose. You spoil it. He'll scream. He'll turn pale and tremble like the coward he is. But he can't get away, Jose, he can't get away! I've got him, Jose! And I'll unbutton his jacket, that hated Yankee uniform. And I'll take this knife and I'll put it right close to his soft, white skin. Then I will press down—down! And you'll hear him scream as it goes in; he'll twist about and shriek, but I will pin him to the floor. And then he will lie there, Jose, and we can watch him die. Ha, Madre di dios, how I hate him!"

The Spaniard's rage had been such that his face grew fairly purple. And he snatched up the knife and started forward toward the cadet.

"How I hate him!" he panted again.

What were the feelings of poor Clif may be imagined; he was perfectly helpless and could only lie still and gaze into the eyes of his deadly foe.

But there was some one else to stop Ignacio.

The sergeant caught him by the arm.

"So, no!" he cried. "Stop."

"What!" panted Ignacio. "Why?"

"They would punish me."

"But they need not know?"

"The others will tell."

"Nonsense."

"But they will."

"What? Cannot a knife kill more than one man. Carramba, I will kill all five."

"But I was ordered to deliver them alive."

Ignacio was nearly frenzied at those objections.

"Jose" he yelled, "you are mad. We can fix it. I will fix it with Blanco. Say they got loose, chewed the ropes, and attacked us. I will swear they did, swear it by all the saints. And I hate that Yankee so, Jose, that I would cut my own flesh to make the story seem more probable. I will say we had a desperate battle—tell them how you saved my life. And you will be promoted. Blanco will believe me, Jose."

But the Spanish soldier shook his head dubiously.

"I dare not," he said. "The captain's last words were to deliver them safely."

"But think of the money, Jose! Think of the money!"

Ignacio fairly ground his teeth with rage over the delay; he was like a wild man.

"Por dios," he cried, "how can you hesitate? It is the chance of your lifetime—of your lifetime!"

The five unfortunate prisoners had not all of them understood those words, but they had no doubt of their meaning. And they lay watching Ignacio feverishly.

It was as if they had been charmed by a serpent, their eyes followed his every motion. They realized that at any moment the cunning villain might leap at them.

But the sergeant, though wavering, still shook his head.

"The men will tell," he objected.

"Here is another hundred for them!" gasped Ignacio. "It is all I have. Por dios, what more?"

There was at least half a minute of agony after that while the man upon whom everything depended wrestled with that temptation. It was a great one, and Clif felt a cold perspiration breaking out all over him as he sat and watched.

But the stolid sergeant was apparently too much of a coward to take the risk. He said no, and Clif gave a gasp.

"Wait and see Blanco," he said. "I do not dare to let you do it."

And though Ignacio blustered and swore and pranced about like a mad man, the soldier was obdurate.

"The risk is too great," he reiterated. "I dare not."

And so Ignacio once more slunk back into a dark corner of the car and fell snarling to himself.

"But I'll have him yet!" Clif heard him hiss. "I'll have him yet. Just wait till we get to Havana."

CHAPTER XIV.

BESSIE STUART.

The event to which Ignacio was looking forward with so much pleasure was not long in taking place.

The trip by the railroad lasted about half an hour only.

Ignacio would hardly have had more than time to carry out his dastardly purpose before the train arrived. The car came slowly to a stop and the sergeant got up and opened the door.

"Here we are," said he. "And I am glad."

Ignacio was apparently glad, too, since he had failed in his first plan. He sprang up eagerly and watched the removal of the prisoners.

The sergeant untied the Americans' feet and gruffly ordered them to march. With the soldiers before and behind they were led rapidly through the streets of Havana.

If the arrival of those prisoners in a small town created excitement, one may well imagine that the big capital turned out a crowd to watch them; but there was almost no demonstration against them, for the party hurried along rapidly. And Ignacio did not try any of his tricks; he knew that his chance would soon come, and he waited patiently.

Clif gazed about him as he walked. He was listless and hopeless, but he could not help feeling an interest in the city he had heard so much of and which he had been so busily helping to blockade.

But he had little chance to look about. He was marching down a long street crowded with Spaniards of all sizes and shades. And then suddenly before a dark, heavy-looking building, the guards came to a halt.

There was a heavy iron door in front of it that opened slowly.

"March in," said the sergeant.

And the prisoners, with bayonets at their backs, were forced up the steps and into the building.

The door shut again with a dull iron clang that sounded like a death knell to Clif.

Ignacio entered, too. He seemed to have the privilege of going where he chose; the sentries who were guarding that door asked him no questions.

It was apparently some sort of a military jail to which they had been taken. Down a long stone corridor they were marched, and then halted in front of a door.

The sergeant entered, and Ignacio after him. The rest waited outside.

It must have been at least fifteen minutes before anything more occurred. Then the sergeant came out, and ordered the prisoners to enter.

Clif, as the officer, entered first, and he found himself facing a tall, military looking Spaniard with a resplendent uniform and an air of authority. Who he was Clif had no idea, but he was evidently in command of the place.

He was a dark, savage-looking man, and his brows were drawn down as he frowned upon the prisoners.

And Clif was not surprised.

"He's had Ignacio to tell him about us," he thought to himself.

Ignacio was standing just behind the officer. There was a grin on his face and a look of delight; he rubbed his hands gleefully as he watched what transpired.

The Spanish officer glared at his prisoners sternly. Clif's bearing was quiet and dignified.

"So you are the officer who commanded the Yankee pigs?" growled the man.

"I am an American naval cadet," was the response.

The Spaniard said nothing more for a moment, but continued his piercing look.

"You put on a bold front," he said at last. "You must have looked differently when you were running away."

The remark required no answer, and got none. Clif did not mean to bandy words with the officer; if he wanted to taunt him he was welcome to do so.

"We treat our prisoners more politely," he thought, "but I suppose this is the Spanish way."

Meanwhile the officer went on.

"You will be less impudent later on," he snarled, "when you learn what is in store for you. You've no idea, I presume."

"I understood that I was a prisoner of war," was the American's quiet answer. "And I understood that Spain considered itself a civilized nation."

The Spaniard laughed softly.

"A prisoner of war," he chuckled. "So you really expect to be treated as such—and after what you have done!"

"What have I done?" asked Clif.

Ignacio's eyes began to dance at that; for the officer turned toward him.

"This gentleman," said the officer, "is one of our trusted agents. And I have learned from him of your villainy."

Clif was not in the least surprised at that. It was just what he had looked for.

"I should be pleased to learn also, if I may, what has this trusted agent told you?"

As he said that, he turned toward the grinning Ignacio.

But it was the officer who continued speaking.

"I suppose you wish to deny everything," said he. "But I assure you it will do not the least good in the world."

"I presume not," escaped Clif's lips.

The Spaniard frowned angrily, but he went on without a change of tone.

"You were captured, if I understand it truly, from a merchantman which you ran upon the rocks in order to prevent one of our vessels from recapturing her?"

"That is true," Clif said.

"And you must have thought it quite a smart trick! But according to this man here, you previously had some fighting with our vessel. Would you mind telling me about it?"

"I would not," said Clif. "We were steaming toward Key West, myself and these four men being a prize crew from the gunboat Uncas. We were hailed from the darkness by another vessel——"

"Ah! And what was the name of the vessel?"

"I do not know."

"Did you not ask?"

"I did. But she answered falsely. She pretended to be an American vessel——"

The Spaniard gave a sneer.

"So that is the yarn you mean to tell," he laughed.

"That is what occurred," said Clif, quickly. "If you have heard otherwise you have been told a lie. And my men will bear me out in the statement."

"Indeed! I do not doubt it."

There was fine sarcasm in that tone; but Clif did not heed it.

"Would you mind telling me what this fellow Ignacio has said?" he inquired.

"He says," responded the other, "that the vessel announced herself as a Spaniard, and called on you to surrender. You did so; and then when the boat's crew came aboard you shot two of them and steamed away. Is that so, Ignacio?"

"It is," snarled the "agent." "I will take my oath upon it."

It was of course a lie; and it made Clif's blood boil. The Spanish vessel had deceived them and tried to capture them by stealth. The men of the Spanish boat's crew had been shot while trying to hold up the American.

But Clif had expected that Ignacio would tell such a tale, and so he was not surprised. The offense with which the lad found himself charged was a terrible one, and he realized that he could be hanged for it.

Yet what was he to do?

"I fear," he said to the Spaniard, "that it will do me little good to deny this story."

"That is true," said the other, promptly.

And his cruel eyes gleamed as he watched the prisoner.

"Do you deny the shooting?" he demanded.

"No," said Clif, "I do not."

"You find it easier to say that the men pretended to be Americans."

"I find it easier because it is truer," was the cadet's answer.

And then there were several moments of silence while the three actors of this little drama watched each other eagerly.

Ignacio was fairly beside himself with triumph. He could scarcely keep himself quiet, and under his bushy eyebrows, his dark eyes gleamed triumphantly.

He had played his trump card. And he had his victim where he wanted him at last. To watch him under the torture of his present position was almost as good as to watch him under the torture of the knife.

For what could he do? He might bluster and protest (all to Ignacio's glee) but nobody would believe him.

For Ignacio knew that the Spanish officer was glad enough to believe the story the spy told him. His prejudice and his hatred of Americans would turn the scale.

And it would be fine to punish a Yankee pig for such a crime as this.

As for Clif, he was filled with a kind of dull despair; he knew the odds against him, and realized that his struggles would be those of a caged animal. He had done nothing but his duty and the law of nations would have justified him. But Ignacio's lie upon that one small point (of what the Spanish gunboat had done) was enough to make him liable to death.

The officer seemed to realize the smallness of difference, for he turned to Ignacio.

"Are you perfectly sure," he demanded, "that you heard our vessel announce her identity?"

"I am, senor."

"And what was her name?"

Clif's eyes brightened at that; he thought Ignacio would be caught there.

But the cunning fellow was prepared, and answered instantly.

"The Regina."

He had chosen the name of a Spanish gunboat he knew to be at sea; and the ruse worked.

"What more can you expect?" demanded the officer of Clif.

And then the cadet looked up to make the last effort for his life.

"As I have told you," he said, "this fellow's story is false. And now I will tell you why he has done it. He has long been an enemy of mine, and he is making an effort to ruin me. I foiled him——"

"If you are going to tell me about that attempt of his to kill your Yankee admiral," interrupted the officer, "I know it already."

And Ignacio gave a chuckle of glee.

"In fact," the officer added, "I have learned of all your adventures, young man. And I have no doubt you consider yourself quite a hero after what you have done against Spain. But you will live to regret it, I think."

And Clif saw that he had nothing to gain by pursuing that tack any further; he was silent, for he knew nothing more to do. The Spaniard went on:

"I know also of another affair of yours," he added. "It seems that your pig government sent a naval officer over to see that bandit robber Gomez. And our friend here, Ignacio, was leading him into our camp. I believe that was it, was it not, Ignacio?"

"It was, senor, and this Yankee here met us———"

"And wounded you and rescued the officer, with the aid of some of the robber's men, and that girl you told me about."

"Exactly," said Ignacio.

"What was her name?" the other continued. "Stuart, I think. We will soon manage to stop her tricks, I fancy."

Clif had been listening to their conversation without any particular interest. But suddenly as he heard that last speech his face flushed crimson and he half staggered back.

"Bessie Stuart!" he gasped, under his breath.

The Spanish officer was looking at him and he laughed as he saw the American's thunderstruck expression.

"Ha! ha!" he chuckled, "so you are interested in her, are you? A sweetheart, perhaps, hey?"

Clif did not answer that; he was staring at the man in horror. Stop her! What in the world could he mean? What could he know about Bessie Stuart?

The girl was a dear friend of Clif's who had come to Cuba to hunt for a relative of hers.

Clif had left her under the protection of Gomez; and that was the last he had heard of her.

And here was the brutal Spaniard mentioning her. How had he and how had the villainous Ignacio learned about her?

It was small wonder that Clif started back; Bessie Stuart was the dearest friend he had.

Meanwhile the Spaniard was leering at him.

"The Yankee pig seems worried," he said. "If that girl is his sweetheart, he did not do wisely to leave her with the bandit Gomez. Did he, Ignacio?"

"No, senor," was that person's grinning response.

"For she will soon be somebody else's sweetheart," chuckled the other.

That was too much. Clif had held himself back, for he did not wish those cruel men to know he could torment him.

But at that last remark he could no longer restrain his anxiety. He sprang toward the Spanish captain with a pleading look on his face.

"Tell me!" he cried. "Tell me—where is she?"

The other's lip curled sneeringly as he stared at him.

"You are very much interested," said he. "Well, to be sure, the girl is pretty—pretty as I ever saw, unfortunately for her. But you may see her again. I expect—she is likely to be in the same prison with you."

Every drop of blood left Clif's face at those terrible words. Bessie Stuart in prison!

"Merciful providence!" he gasped.

And then once more he sprang toward the Spaniard, a look on his face, a look of agony that would have touched a heart of stone.

"For Heaven's sake, sir," he gasped, "tell me!"

"Tell you what?"

"Is she in Havana?"

The Spaniard laughed softly.

Then he nodded toward Ignacio.

"Ask him," he said. "He keeps track of such people for us. She has been here some time now; and people who get into our prisons don't—ha! ha! they don't get out in a hurry, do them, Ignacio?"

"No, senor."

"And then she is very pretty, too," added the officer, with a laugh.

To the agony those remarks were raising in the mind of poor Clif those two brutal men seemed quite insensible. Or perhaps they were teasing him.

But if so, the officer had enough then, for he turned upon his heel impatiently.

"Enough of this nonsense," he said. "You need not worry about your sweetheart, for you will probably be dead by to-morrow."

And the man turned to the soldiers.

"Those four prisoners," he said, pointing to the sailors, "will be kept here for the present. They will probably be exchanged in a few days. We do not blame them for the crime this officer here committed. As for him, he will probably be sent over to Morro Castle to-night."

And then the file of soldiers closed about the dazed cadet and led him out of the room. He was scarcely able to walk by himself.

The last sound that he heard as he left the room was the fiendish chuckle of the triumphant Ignacio.

CHAPTER XV.

IN MORRO CASTLE.

That certainly was a day of triumph for the vindictive Spaniard. Not only Clif Faraday was made wretched, but there was his friend, too, and each a thousand times more unhappy because of the misfortune of the other.

Clif as he went out of that room was almost dazed; he could think of nothing. He scarcely heard the sailors sadly bidding him good-by.

Nor did he notice anything else until he heard the clang of a door behind him, he realized then from the darkness and silence about him that he was alone in one of the cells of the prison.

It was not for himself that the poor cadet feared. He could have marched out without flinching and faced a dozen rifles aimed at his heart.

But it was for Bessie Stuart, fallen into the hands of these brutal men. The fate that was before her was enough to make Clif wish her dead.

He racked his brains trying to think of how she could have come to Havana; could she have been captured in a battle? And what had Ignacio to do with it?

But poor Clif knew nothing, and could think of nothing except that she was here, and he powerless to aid her.

His own fate was terrible enough, though he hardly thought of that.

He was to be sent at night to Morro.

Many indeed were the unfortunates who had gone to take that sea trip in the darkness and never come back—and sometimes not reached their destination either. It was a terrible journey, that short ride across Havana Bay.

But the cadet did not even stop to realize that. He had but one thought, and that he kept repeating over and over to himself in a state of confusion and despair. He never moved from his one position on the floor; and the hours flew by unheeded.

Once and once only the heavy door of the cell was opened and that by a man who shoved in a pitcher of water and a dish of food. He must have thought the prisoner asleep.

And as a fact, Clif was half unconscious; he was too dazed to think of anything. He had no hope and no chance of life, and nothing to think of except that Bessie Stuart was captured and he could not aid her.

So the long day wore by; it was as a man waking from a deep sleep that the wretched American looked up when the door of that cell was opened again. He found that the hours had flown by, and that the time for the trip to Morro had come.

If Clif had cared about anything then he would have shivered with horror at that moment, for it was surely gruesome and uncanny enough.

Three men there were, dark, silent, shadowy figures who entered the damp cell. The only light they had was from a dark lantern, which they flashed upon the solitary prisoner.

They found him still lying on the floor, but he raised up to look at them, his haggard, tortured face shining white in the rays of the lantern.

"Get up," commanded one of the men, in a low, muffled voice. "Get up."

The face of the speaker was shrouded in darkness, but Clif recognized the voice, and a cold chill shot over him.

"Ignacio again!" he gasped.

Yes. And Clif thought that this was the last—that Ignacio had gained his purpose. The task of murder was left to him.

But there was no chance of resistance. Clif felt the cold muzzle of a revolver pressed to his head, and so he put the thought away.

One of the men snapped a pair of handcuffs about his wrists, as if to make sure of him in case the ropes were not strong enough. And then one of them seized him by each arm and Ignacio stepped behind with the lantern.

And so out of the cell they marched and down the long corridor and out of the building into the open air.

Clif had chance for but one deep breath of it. A moment later he was shoved into a wagon that was in front of the door.

There he was seated between one of the men and the chuckling Ignacio. The other man was driving and they rattled off down the street.

Where they were going the unfortunate victim had no idea. Perhaps to some lonely spot where Ignacio could torture him to his fiendish heart's content! But there was no use in making an outcry.

And Clif realized it and sat perfectly silent. He would give his enemies no more satisfaction than he could help.

Clif did not think that it could be the trip to Morro that was before him; it was too early for such a deed of darkness. If he were dropped overboard upon the way some one might see it.

But as it actually happened, Morro was his destination. And he really reached Morro, too. Perhaps the city jail was not considered strong enough for such a villain as he.

And the carriage stopped at a wharf. A small launch was waiting there, and the party boarded her and were swept across to the other side in a very short while.

So in a short while the walls of Havana's strongest dungeon shut upon Clif Faraday. He was a prisoner in Morro, famous or infamous, for its deeds of horror.

For it was in this place, as Clif knew, that all the torture and cruelty of the Spanish nature had been wreaked upon the unfortunate Cubans or Americans who fell into the hands of Weyler. It was here that Ruiz had been murdered, and hundreds of wretches besides—their name and fate being hidden forever by the walls of that horrible place.

And Clif was going then under the guidance of Ignacio. It was plain that the fiendish man had secured his purpose, for he was in command of the little party. And it was his to decide what was to be done with Clif.

How the man had secured that privilege from the authorities Clif could not hope to know. That he had gotten it as a reward for some deed of darkness he did not doubt.

Perhaps it was for capturing Bessie Stuart, was the thought that flashed over the lad.

Again when the black, silent walls of Morro loomed up before them and the great gate opened nobody asked any questions of Ignacio. He showed a note, and it passed him from sentry to sentry; and the party passed down a flight of stairs into a cold, damp, stone corridor black as night.

Poor Clif could not help but think of his own fate then. Ignacio's cruelty and hatred were such that no torture would be terrible enough for him. And he seemed to have his prisoner entirely to his own discretion.

The great vault through which they were going echoed dimly to the footsteps of the party. They seemed to be down in a sort of a cellar, and they were winding their way through secret passages in almost absolute darkness.

But Ignacio knew the way—probably the fellow had been in those gloomy dungeons before.

He stopped suddenly and flashed the lantern upon a rusty iron door. It was solid and heavy, but Ignacio took a key from his pocket and unlocked it.

It swung back, creaking dismally upon its hinges. And Ignacio flashed the light of his lantern in.

He staggered back quite white with fright as he did so. For there was a series of thumping, shuffling sounds, and a shrill noise that made his blood run cold.

But in a moment he again stepped forward, laughing under his breath.

"Por dios!" he exclaimed. "The rats! They must be hungry!"

And he stepped into the room. His foot splashed into a small puddle of water on the reeking, earthen floor. But he pressed on, flashing his lantern about the granite walls.

It was a tiny black cavern into which he had come.

There was a stone bench at one side of the horrible place, and in the wall by it a heavy ring and a thick iron chain.

It was but a minute more before Clif's ankles were locked firmly in the ring, and then he was utterly helpless.

For but a moment Ignacio stood looking at him, flashing the lantern full in his face. And then he turned and motioned to the two men.

Without a word they faced about and stole away. They went out of the door, and Ignacio, trembling all over with his fiendish eagerness, shut the great iron barrier and locked it.

And then with a hoarse cry of rage he faced about.

Clif Faraday was alone with his deadly and merciless foe!

CHAPTER XVI.

IN THE DUNGEON VAULTS.

Ignacio was a horrible object to contemplate at that moment, and it was but little wonder that Clif turned sick and faint as he watched him.

The man seemed fairly turned into a devil then. He seemed insane. He was alone, absolutely alone, with his victim. And no one under heaven could stop him. He had the key himself! And he had his prisoner iron-bound and helpless!

For several moments the man fairly danced about the place, yelling as if to prove to his hated foe that there was no care for anything any more.

And then suddenly he made a leap at him.

He crouched in front of him until his gleaming eyes shone into his face, and his hot breath could be felt. His claw-like fingers he seemed scarcely able to keep away from Clif.

"Yankee!" he hissed, in a wild voice. "Yankee, do you know where you are?"

The fiendish man saw the white look on his victim's face; and he laughed.

"You do know!" he cried. "You do know! Ha! ha! You are in Morro, deep in the lowest vault! And no soul can come near you—near you—hear me?"

He struck him in the face as if to draw his attention.

"Listen; yes, stare at me! I don't wonder you quake. You have defied me— ha, ha! You have ruined all my plans, but I've got you now. And, oh, how I will pay you back, how I will twist you and tear you! You shall pay for everything. And you may shriek and scream and no one will know it more than if you did not. Listen!"

And again from sheer bravado Ignacio raised his voice and shouted. The sound died in the grave-like cell—the granite and the iron shut it in.

"You see!" panted Ignacio. "Not a soul heard! And you are mine. Ah, they hate you and they like me, for I told them about that girl. Ha, ha! You wince!"

Ignacio's face was almost touching Clif's as he hissed that.

"You can't get away!" he yelled. "And, oh, the things that I shall do to you! I've got instruments up stairs to tear you to pieces, burn your eyes out—but never kill you, oh, no! And all night you will scream, and all to-morrow, if I choose. And I will watch you—I and the rats. And the rats will eat you, too!"

As if to add horror to the devil's gleeful statement, a huge slimy rat ran across Clif's body just then; it made him shiver all over.

And Ignacio danced about as he saw him.

"Ha, ha!" he cried. "You begin! But wait till I start—wait till you begin to feel some agony—till I begin to tear your eyes out! Then will you yell? When I get through with you—ha, ha!—when you are dead, perhaps weeks from now, you won't mind the rats any more! You may stay in here in this grave for the Yankees to find if they capture Morro as they say they will. Oh, I will make it a sight for them!"

Clif could not have stood the strain of that horrible ordeal much longer; he would have fainted away.

But then the fiendish Spaniard's impatience got the better of him. And he turned and crept toward the door again.

"I will get the instruments," he whispered, hoarsely. "The torture instruments. Santa Maria, what things they are! And how you will shriek!"

A moment later he turned the key and stepped out. He shut the door and locked it. And Clif was left alone in all the blackness and horror of that slimy place.

Never as long as he lives will he forget the agony of that long wait. He sat straining his ears and listening for the first sign of the fiend's return. He knew that he might come back any instant and begin his horrible, merciless tormenting.

Clif knew that man for a devil incarnate. He would sooner have looked for mercy in a hyena.

For Ignacio was of the race of the Inquisition; and of the horrors of the Inquisition this was a fair sample.

The wretched American knew that he was alone and that he could look for no rescue. He was buried in the very centre of the earth—or the centre of hades.

And his cries would be heard only by Ignacio.

Clif knew also that the frenzied villain would make haste, that he would come back panting and eager. Appalled, half dazed, he sat and listened.

The first thing he would hear would be the grating of the key; and then would come horrors inconceivable.

Seconds were years at that time. Clif thought that his hair would turn white from the suspense.

And then suddenly he gave a gasp.

There he was!

Yes, the key was sliding in. And now it was turning!

And then slowly the door was opened—groaning and creaking.

Clif imagined the dark, crouching figure. He had left the lantern behind while these deeds of darkness went on.

The tomb-like cell was absolutely black, and Clif could not see one thing. But he heard the door shut, heard the key turned. He shivered as in an ague fit.

Above the noise of the scampering rats he heard a soft, stealthy footstep as the man crept across the floor.

And then came the scratching sound of a hand running along the wall. He was feeling for him!

And a moment later Clif gave an involuntary cry as he felt the hand touch his face.

Perfectly motionless and paralyzed he sat and fancied what might be going on in the blackness after that. He felt, the hand pass downward along his body, felt it fumbling at the manacles that bound his ankles to the wall of the cell.

Then to his surprise, his consternation, he heard a key softly turned.

What happened then almost took away his breath.

The iron fell off.

He was loose!

"Can he be going to take me elsewhere?" Clif gasped.

But he nerved himself for one thing; gathered his muscles for it. Before Ignacio secured him again he would get a kick, one that would almost kill him.

Eagerly Clif waited, to see what would happen next.

But what did happen was more startling and incredible yet; he could scarcely believe his senses.

For he felt the hands running down his arm. They fumbled at his wrists for an instant.

And then with a clatter the handcuffs dropped to the ground!

"Merciful heavens!" Clif thought to himself. "Can he be insane?"

For a moment he actually thought so; then it flashed over him that perhaps the fiend was torturing him with the most horrible of all tortures—hope.

"He'll wish he hadn't!" Clif gasped, as he braced his muscles.

But that was not the true solution of the mystery; there were stranger things yet stranger and stranger.

The only things that bound Clif now were the ropes that had held his wrists at first. He tugged at them, but in vain.

There was a moment's silent pause. And then to Clif's unutterable consternation he heard another sound, a sound from across the room—a low, grating sound!

It left him breathless.

Some one else was coming into the cell!

And with one rush the true state of affairs swept over Clif.

"This isn't Ignacio!" he panted.

And a moment later he received proof positive of that fact. For again the hand stole down his arms and there came a couple of quick slashing cuts that hurt his wrists more than the ropes.

But seconds were precious then. In one of them Clif's hands were free.

And his pulses leaped as he felt the knife thrust into his palm. He clutched it, and he heard one word whispered—in English:

"Fight!"

And then the dark figure stole swiftly over to the other side of the cell. It was at the same instant that the door was opened and the light of a lantern flashed in.

It was Ignacio returning!

CHAPTER XVII.

OUT OF THE DUNGEON.

The furious Spaniard came in like some wild beast, fairly gnashing his teeth and snarling to himself in his rage.

Clif had but a moment, but he was quick to think; he sprang back to his old position, slipping his feet into the iron ring and putting his hands behind him.

And Ignacio never noticed any difference, in fact he did not look at Clif until he had set down the lantern and shut the heavy door.

He turned the key again and then faced about; touching low and muttering to himself, he stole swiftly across the floor.

And his gleaming eyes flashed into Clif's face.

"Yankee!" he hissed, "I am back. Do you hear me? Ha, ha!"

As if to make sure that he heard him he struck him once more across the face.

"Listen!" he cried. "Ha, ha!—and tremble."

Clif's blood rose at that blow, but he held himself back and watched and waited.

That was a moment of peril for the treacherous Spaniard; what would have been his terror may be imagined, had he known the victim into whose eyes he was glaring was clutching in one hand a sharp knife, ready at any instant to plunge it into him.

But the fellow had no idea of his peril; he was at the very height of his triumph and his dark, beady eyes gleamed ferociously out of the shadows of that damp and silent vault.

But he must have noticed that some of the color had come back into Clif's face.

"You are still defiant," he cried. "You still do not tremble. But wait—wait till you begin to feel what I have for you. Did you see those iron things I brought in? Ha, ha! There is one I will fasten about your forehead and draw it tight till your very brain bursts. And then will you like it? Hey? Will you turn pale then? Will you scream? Ha, ha!—and I shall dance around you and watch you. Will you be sorry you interfered with me then?"

Ignacio might have taunted his victim that way for hours, but he was too eager and impatient. He whirled about and sprang toward the door.

"Santa Maria!" he panted. "I will get it! I will begin! I must hear him yelling!"

And he snatched up something from the floor and taking the lantern in his other hand bounded back toward Clif.

"Are you ready?" he exclaimed. "Yankee pig, begin to scream!"

And he flashed the lantern's light upon him.

That was the crisis of the situation; for as the Spaniard looked he made the appalling discovery that his victim's feet were untied.

And he staggered back, dazed.

"Por dios!" he gasped.

And that exclamation was his last sound.

Clif had nerved himself for the spring; for he knew that Ignacio might have a revolver and that no risks could be taken.

But at that instant a dark, shadowy form rose up behind Ignacio.

And one of his own iron instruments was raised above his head. It came down with a hissing sound, and then a heavy thud.

And Ignacio dropped without a groan, without even a quiver. He lay perfectly motionless. His villainy was at an end.

Clif had sprung up as he saw that, and he gave a gasp of joy. Then he sprang toward his deliverer.

The shadowy stranger took no notice of him at first, but stooped and picked up the lantern, turning the light of it upon Ignacio.

The villain's face was fixed in a look of horror; it made both Clif and the stranger shudder.

The latter regarded it for a moment silently. The cadet could not see, but he was fingering a knife, as if undecided what to do.

Who his mysterious deliverer was Clif had no idea. The single ray from the lantern did not furnish light enough for him to see anything; and the person had spoken but one word—"Fight."

But the cadet's heart was full of gratitude; he sprang toward the stranger.

"Who are you?" he cried. "I owe my life to you—let me thank you!"

But the other motioned him back, and then for a few moments there was a silence, while both stared at Ignacio's silent form.

When the stranger moved it was to point toward the door.

"Go," said he to Clif, in a low, whispering voice. "Go; we will leave him here."

And with that the mysterious person unlocked the great iron barrier and followed Clif out. The door clanged upon that ghastly scene, and Clif Faraday gave a sigh of relief.

Yet there was so much before him that he soon forgot that hideous nightmare.

For where was he going? And who was this stranger? And why had he rescued him? And what did he mean to do to Clif?

Nothing could be learned in that dark corridor, for Clif could see no more there than inside of the room. But the stranger stumbled on and Clif followed.

They came to an iron ladder, leading up to the floor above. Up that the man went, the cadet following; that took them to another long stone passage, dark as ever.

On they went, turning and winding about, but still not hesitating. And then suddenly the man halted in front of a grated door.

The key was in the lock and the door opened promptly as he turned it.

"Enter," said he.

Clif went in, and he heard the door shut behind him. It flashed over him then that he had only been taken to another cell.

But when he whirled about he saw that the stranger had entered, too. The dark figure brushed past him and went across the room. A moment afterward Clif heard him in the act of striking a match.

And then the light of a lamp lit up the little room. By it the eager cadet could see his rescuer, and he stared anxiously.

Further secrecy seemed not intended. The stranger faced about and each looked at the other steadfastly.

What the mysterious man saw was a tall, handsome American in a blue uniform, his face rather pale.

Clif in turn saw also a man in a blue uniform; he had to take but one glance to see that he was a lieutenant in the Spanish army.

He was a tall, finely proportioned man, rather young, and with a slight dark mustache. He had the dark skin and the features of a Spaniard; but Clif thought he had never seen a finer looking military man.

For a moment Clif gazed at him in silence. Then he stepped toward him.

"Tell me, sir," he said. "Why have you done this?"

The officer answered in a low, quiet voice:

"You will soon know," said he. "Do not be impatient."

"You have saved me from a horrible fate," said the cadet, his voice choking. "I do not know how to thank you."

"Do not try," answered the other. "You have some one else to thank."

And then he became silent again, watching Clif. He seemed to be very much interested in him, from the way he studied the American's face. And once he gave a slight sigh.

Clif looked at him in surprise; but the man turned away, and he went toward the door.

"I will return soon," said he, again in that quiet, firm voice. "Wait here."

There was nothing for Clif to do but wait; for when the door shut he was locked in the cell.

That man's action was a mysterious one indeed. It left the cadet plenty to think of. He saw now where he got the keys. He was evidently one of the officers in charge of the castle.

But why had he done it? Clif was utterly baffled before that question.

But it was not for very long; he soon learned, and in a startling and unexpected way.

Clif had not noticed it, but there was another door to that cell. It was behind him, leading to a small room in the rear.

While he stood there motionless and lost in thought waiting for the Spaniard's return, that door was silently opened, and a figure stood watching him.

And then suddenly it stepped out and came across the room.

The cadet heard it then, and whirled about. He took one glance.

And then he staggered back with a cry of consternation.

It was Bessie Stuart!

For one instant the two stood and stared at each other as if to make sure that their eyes did not deceive them. And then, with a cry of delight that came from his very soul, Clif sprang toward the girl.

Bessie Stuart looked as if she had been through some terrible ordeal, for her face was pale; the emotion of meeting Clif almost overcame her, and she burst into tears upon his shoulder.

Clif himself was so dazed that he hardly knew what to think. He caught the girl in his arms to keep her from falling.

"Bessie," he cried, "how on earth did you get here?"

The cadet's brain was in a whirl at that moment. He began to see what the Spaniard meant when he said it was for some other person's sake that he had rescued Clif. It was for her sake!

And it must have been by some terrible sacrifice that she had saved him from the torture.

"Bessie!" he cried. "Tell me—that officer. What——"

The girl looked up through her tears.

"S-sh!" she exclaimed. "It is all right. Wait."

And at that instant Clif heard a key turn in the door, and knew that it was the man returning.

Clif gazed into the girl's face and he saw a look of joy upon it that partially reassured him; then he looked up and saw that the Spanish lieutenant had entered and was watching them.

In his quiet way he studied the faces of the two; he saw the look of happiness on Bessie Stuart's face, and he must have known that it was because she had met the cadet again.

Clif saw him press his lips together resolutely. The cadet was watching him with the intensest anxiety, for he hoped in that man's actions to read the meaning of this mystery.

But the Spaniard's handsome face showed little emotion, though his chest heaved and fell as he stood there.

And then suddenly he stepped forward toward the two.

"I have brought it, Miss Stuart," he said, with a dignified bow.

He held out a heavy cloth cape, which the girl flung over her shoulders; then, leaning on Clif's arm, she stepped toward the door.

"I am ready," she said.

And without another word the officer turned and led the way out of the cell.

He shut the door and locked it behind him and then went on down the corridor.

Clif was mystified beyond expression, but he asked no questions. The three went on silently. Bessie Stuart was so weak that she had to be half carried.

They had gone but a short way down the long passage before they met a sentry with a gun upon his shoulder; he glanced at them inquiringly.

But the lieutenant was not one who could be asked for explanations, and the soldier saluted and passed on.

They passed through two heavily grated doors, each guarded in a similar way. But still not a word was spoken.

And then suddenly Clif saw the passage broaden out into a wide hall, and a moment later he came to what he knew to be the great door by which he had first entered.

There were two men standing on guard there, either sentries or jailers. Clif could not see which. The party came to a halt.

"Garcia," said the lieutenant, "these are two prisoners, Americans, whom I have been directed to take across the bay."

The man saluted and bowed respectfully.

"Have you the order?" he inquired.

"I have not. The commander had no time to give one to me. There is some hurry in the matter, I believe."

"It is somewhat irregular, lieutenant."

"I will assume full responsibility," said the other, quietly.

The man scanned the two prisoners closely.

"They are not even bound," he objected.

"I will assume full responsibility," said the officer again.

He spoke rather sharply; and without another word the man hastened to swing back the door.

And the three stepped out of that black prison into the open air and under the broad sky of heaven.

And the lieutenant turned toward the two Americans.

"You are free," he said, quietly. "Fly for your lives!"

CHAPTER XVIII.

CLIF FARADAY'S SACRIFICE.

It is needless to say that Clif stared at the man in amazement. But an instant before he had heard him state that he was willing to assume responsibility for them as prisoners.

And now he was saying that they were free!

But there was no time to ask any questions. Bessie Stuart was clinging to Clif's arm and urging him on.

"Have you got some place to hide us?" she inquired anxiously of the officer.

"It is hardly likely that I would leave you here," was the other's quiet answer. "Come."

He led them away from the prison. A short distance off there was standing a small closed carriage.

"Here it is," said the Spaniard. "Step in."

Clif helped the girl inside; and then entered himself. He expected the officer to follow, but he did not; he clambered up with the driver.

And the carriage rattled off down the road.

Clif saw his chance then. He turned eagerly toward the girl.

"Bessie!" he cried, "for Heaven's sake, tell me what this all means. Who is this man? And why is he setting us at liberty?"

The girl sank back weakly in the seat.

"I will tell you the story, Clif," she said. "There is plenty of time, for we have a long ways to go."

"He is ruining himself for us!" Clif exclaimed. "For you! Why he will be court-martialed and shot if he lets us get away."

"I know it," groaned the girl, choking down a sob. "I know it. We talked it all over beforehand. But it was a question of his life or mine."

"Are you sure he is not tricking us?" gasped Clif—"kidnapping us?"

The girl smiled sadly.

"You do not understand the circumstances," she said. "Wait, and let me tell you."

Clif missed in his friend the old self-reliant manner that she had always had; she was nervous and weak, and it was plain that she was not well.

And Clif was trembling all over with anxiety as he watched her.

"Go on!" he cried. "Tell me. How did you get here, in the first place?"

"You left me with Gomez," began the girl, taking a deep breath. "I did not stay very long, for he was marching about, and I could not stand the strain. He wanted me to go to one of the Cuban villages in the interior where his family was; but I was anxious to get back to the United States. And so I came here to Havana——"

"To Havana!"

"Yes, for I thought no one would know me."

"And Ignacio saw you?"

"Yes, and recognized me. But that was only the other day."

"Where were you meanwhile?"

"I had a letter to the British consul, and I stayed at his home. There was so much suffering in this city that I couldn't stay idle. I used to go to the hospitals to take care of the poor people, the Cubans. And that was how I met Lieutenant Hernandez."

"Who is he?"

"He is the man who has rescued us. He had been hurt in the Matanzas bombardment, and one of his arms was terribly cut. I took care of him—he was there because the military hospitals were crowded. And, Clif, I—I—I guess he fell in love with me."

The girl flushed as she said that.

"I should not tell, perhaps," she went on, hastily. "But it is your right to know this, and you would not understand if I didn't tell you. Clif, he asked me to marry him."

Clif started and turned pale.

"Bessie!" he exclaimed in horror.

The thought of that girl's marrying the Spanish officer was terrible. It flashed over him that that was the reason why the rescue had been attempted.

"Oh, Bessie!" he cried again.

Clif had never breathed a word of love to her in his life. But all through their trying journey through Cuba he had protected her, fairly worshiped her. And he had thought she understood his feelings.

And now he thought that he had lost her—she had promised to be that officer's wife! It was no wonder that he felt his hands grow icy.

His heart fairly stood still as he waited for the girl to go on.

"I will tell you," said Bessie. "You must know in the first place that this man is a gentleman, a hero in fact. You will understand it when I tell you what he has done."

"Go on."

"When he left the hospital, as I say, he begged me to marry him—declared he would resign from the army if I would."

The girl was breathing hard as she continued; it was evident that the subject pained her.

"I felt so sorry for him," she said, in a low, trembling voice. "For I think it has nearly broken his heart. I refused him. I told him that I liked him, but I did not, I could not marry him. I had been kind to him because he was ill. He swore that he would die for me—and, Clif, I think he has nearly carried out his promise."

Bessie Stuart choked down a sob.

"I refused him," she said again. "And then came the horrible Ignacio. He saw me on the street. That was three days ago; and that same day I was placed under arrest."

"What for?"

"Why, Ignacio knew that I had been fighting with Gomez; you know we had a fight with some Spaniards when he was along. And so there was no chance for me. The British consul did all he could for me, but there was no hope. I could not deny the charges. And, oh, Clif, I have had a frightful time. I was taken over to those horrible dungeons in Morro. And I was sentenced to death. I was to be taken out and shot to-morrow."

The girl stopped for a few moments to recover her composure.

"And how did you find out about me?" asked Clif.

"I will tell you," said Bessie. "But first I must go on about this Lieutenant Hernandez. I did not know it, but he was stationed over here. And when he found out what had happened to me he managed to come in to see me."

And then Clif felt able to complete that story.

"I suppose," said he, "that he offered to free you if you would marry him."

Bessie Stuart smiled sadly.

"You do not know the man," said she. "I will tell you what he did say. I can almost hear him saying it."

"What?"

"'Miss Stuart,' he said, 'you have said you do not love me. And I think you love some one else—I do not know whom; but I will not make you unhappy by urging you any more. I might take advantage of your present position to get you to promise to marry me. But I will not. If you will be ready to-night I will help you to escape, and prove what I said about dying for you.'"

The girl stopped and sat silent, too much moved to speak. And Clif was too astonished.

That was indeed the act of a noble nature. The cadet saw it all then, why the man had freed them and why he and the girl were both so quiet and sad. Lieutenant Hernandez had given his life for hers.

It was fully a minute before anything more was said. Then Bessie Stuart began again, in a low voice:

"About you," she said. "It was the lieutenant who told me, quite by accident. He said there were five Americans captured, one a cadet, and that he was to be killed. When I asked the name and he told me, I fainted dead away. And I think that hurt the lieutenant more than anything."

"Why?"

"I told him the story, how you had twice rescued me from the Spaniards. And he asked—he asked if you were his rival."

The girl stepped abruptly.

"And you said that I was, I hope," said Clif, quietly.

Most women would have been embarrassed by a question such as that. But Bessie Stuart was not.

There was some of the old-time self-possession in her voice as she responded. She turned and looked fairly into Clif's eyes.

"I know you well enough to speak my mind," she said. "Yes, I told him that you were."

And then the two sat perfectly silent, looking at each other. It was a very few words they had said, but they covered a lifetime of feeling.

In that quiet way and under those strange circumstances Clif had unbosomed his heart; and Bessie Stuart had done the same.

It was the first word that Clif had ever said to indicate how he felt toward her.

For the two sat in silence for a minute or so; and then Clif went on:

"You told this officer that I was his rival," said he; "that you loved me and that I was the only barrier to his hopes?"

"I did," said the girl.

"And he still was willing to save my life?"

"You see what he has done," answered the other. "He said that he loved me, that he would risk his life to make me happy. And here we are."

"But not happy," Clif added, half under his breath.

Then again there was a long silence. One cannot say much when one feels as deeply as those two felt then.

Clif thought of the heroism of that quiet Spanish officer. And his heart went out toward him. He fancied what the man's own feelings must be, the loneliness and the desolation.

He had ruined himself, accepted voluntarily disgrace and a shameful death. And all in order that a woman who had been kind to him might be set free and made happy.

Of the death there could be no doubt. When that officer was caught he would have it to face. And he would face it for the sake of Bessie Stuart.

And moreover, he was aiding Clif, his rival, the one who was robbing him of his heart's desire; he was helping him to freedom so that the cadet, when his work in the war was done, might claim the woman he loved as his reward.

That was heroism; not the noisy kind in the battle, which every one sees and applauds, but the quiet kind that knows it is right and cares for no one else.

Clif felt that he could worship such a man as that.

And it is needless to say that his conscience troubled him. What right had he to accept such a sacrifice?

But the alternative was a terrible one. The lieutenant might flee with them to the United States; and then——

Clif could not finish the thought; it made him shudder.

Just then Bessie Stuart spoke again.

"Clif," she said, "I have something to say to you. And I shall speak plainly, for there is no time to hesitate. I have told you how I feel toward you; I have told you that I loved you. Neither of us would have declared our feelings, I suppose, if it had not been for this situation. But I have been with you for months, and I have never known you to do anything I could not admire. And mine is no childish fancy, Clif, for we have been doing the work of men, you and I. Clif——"

The girl choked back a sob—and then went on:

"We must stop," she said, "stop where we are."

Clif knew what was coming, and he felt his blood surging. Bessie Stuart's hand was in his and it was trembling.

For a moment she could not speak; the words would not come.

But then with that terrible self-command she sometimes displayed, she mastered her emotion and turned to look into her companion's face.

"Clif," she said, "you know what I mean. You must let me marry this officer."

Clif had known, and so he did not move when he heard those awful words. He sat perfectly motionless, almost frozen; he felt the girl's hand turn cold in his.

The carriage rolled on, and for at least one long, long minute there was not a sound. The girl was listening, trembling again; and Clif, half dazed was thinking to himself, thinking again and again of that death knell, "You must let me marry this officer."

And it was true. Clif knew it. It was his duty; and the feeling lingered in his mind that if he had half the heroism of that Spaniard he would have said so long ago.

At last he spoke. His mouth was dry and his voice husky, but he forced the words out.

And they were the right ones.

"Yes," said he, "you must marry him. And we must never meet again."

And then once more came the terrible silence. Bessie Stuart heard him choke down a sob; and her heart was ready to break.

For this cadet was the dearest friend she had. She had been through terrible dangers with him, coming to love him more every day, as she saw the brave man's daring. And no one could ever know now how she felt toward him.

But there was her duty; and though she was nearly ready to faint, she sat perfectly motionless by his side.

And so for two or three minutes they rode on in silence; then suddenly they heard the driver of the carriage stopping his horses.

"We are there," said Clif, in a husky voice.

He turned to look at the girl once more; he found that she was gazing at him, and their eyes met.

There was anguish in both of their faces; Miss Stuart could scarcely see for her tears.

But Clif took her hands in his. All the emotion of his lifetime seemed crowded into that moment. He bent toward her and their lips met in one trembling kiss.

And then with a set look on his face the cadet rose from his seat and opened the door of the carriage, which had stopped.

CHAPTER XIX.

A FAREWELL.

Clif found Lieutenant Hernandez waiting for them to come out. Both he and the driver had descended from the carriage.

It was quite dark where they were, apparently surrounded by a lonely woods. But by such light as there was Clif looked at the officer anxiously.

Now since he had heard that story he was more than anxious to study his face, to see what manner of man this was.

The lieutenant still wore the calm, quiet look; he seemed almost inspired.

"If you will follow me a short distance," he said, "we shall reach a place where we can remain concealed until morning."

He started across the country, after a few words with the driver of the carriage; they had not gone very far before the faint roaring of the breakers on the beach became audible.

"You see," said the Spaniard, "we are near the sea. We are only about four miles from Havana harbor, and you may make an effort to reach the blockading fleet in the morning."

Obviously, it would not do to try it in the darkness. They might be run down or lost or fired on or swept out to sea.

"But it will be daylight in a few hours," said the lieutenant.

And then the three went on in silence until suddenly a small hut loomed up in the darkness.

"It is deserted," said their guide. "We can conceal ourselves there."

And accordingly, they crept through the low doorway, and finding the place covered with straw inside, sat down to wait.

There was no conversation among them, for each one of the trio was wrapped in his own sad thoughts. The place was in absolute darkness, and so they could not see each other.

But Clif was revolving a plan over in his thoughts, and it was not very many minutes before he made up his mind.

He rose to his feet again.

"Excuse me for a while," he said. "I will return."

And with that he hurried out of the hut.

Bessie Stuart knew why he had gone, and after a moment's silence she turned toward the lieutenant.

"My friend has left," she said, "in order that I may have a chance to talk to you."

The officer answered nothing; the girl went on slowly.

"Lieutenant Hernandez," she said "will you answer me a question?"

"What is it?"

"What do you intend to do?"

"How do you mean?"

"I mean that you will be court-martialed if you return to Havana——"

"Yes," said the other, "I know that."

"Do you mean to return there?"

"Such are my plans at present," was the quiet response.

Miss Stuart thought a moment before she began again.

"Lieutenant Hernandez," she said at last, "you have been a hero to-day."

"I have done my best," said the man.

"You have done what few men would have. You have given your life for our safety."

"Yes," answered he, "I have."

"But there are other heroes, Lieutenant Hernandez," said the girl. "You have inspired us two. That is what I wish to speak to you about. I have a better plan than your return to Havana."

"What is it?"

"Come to America with us——"

"And then?"

"Then I will do my best to repay your favor. I will do as you have asked me."

"You mean——"

"I mean that I will marry you the day that we arrive."

The girl said those words in a low, earnest tone. She saw the officer give a start, she even fancied she heard his heart begin to beat louder.

But he said nothing. The two sat as they were in silence. The Spaniard was having his struggle then.

The pause continued for at least five minutes; it was broken only once.

"Does Cadet Faraday know of this?" asked the officer.

"He does," said the girl. "We talked it over in the carriage."

"And he said that he was willing to give you up?"

"He did."

"I am glad that I saved him," muttered the man.

Bessie Stuart was a little puzzled to catch the drift of that last remark. But she soon saw what it meant.

She was quite startled by the decision to which the Spaniard came.

"Miss Stuart," he began, in a low, trembling voice, "this is indeed a reward for my helping you. I cannot tell you how much I appreciate it. It shows me that those I helped were worth helping. And it makes me all the more sorry."

"Sorry?"

"Yes, sorry that it cannot be."

The girl gave a slight gasp.

"What cannot be?"

"I cannot marry you. I will not."

The officer paused for a moment, then he went on.

"It is plain to me," he said, "that you have worshiped this cadet. I do not blame you, after what I have just seen of him. I have heard of his bravery, too, and he is worthy of you—more so than I am. As I say, Miss Stuart, you love him; and you do not love me. You make this proposal to me from a sense of duty, and I cannot think of accepting it. You would never be happy again."

The girl started to protest, but the lieutenant held up his hand to stop her.

"No," he said, "there are more reasons, even stronger ones, I could not think of going to the United States. I could not think of turning traitor to my country. You forget, since I have helped you, that I am still a Spaniard; and while this war continues I shall remain with my countrymen."

"But they will kill you!"

"They may do what they please with me. It is not for me to say. I have done my duty; I will not become a traitor."

The officer was silent for a moment, sadly staring ahead in the darkness.

"You Americans forget how we Spaniards feel," he began slowly. "You think us foolish to fight for a dying country. I know that it is dying; for I am not one of those who blind their eyes and boast. I know that we are bankrupt and disorganized, our men dying, and our enemies closing in on us. We cannot keep up with modern nations. But, Miss Stuart, it is still Spain, my native land; my friends are there, my memories are there. And Spain's enemies are mine."

There was a gleam in the proud Castilian's eyes as he said that; but then he sank back with a sigh.

"It is useless," he said, "foolish, if you will. And I am tired of the struggle, tired of weeping at my country's trials, her follies. I shall be glad to leave. I can die without a murmur. When I go back to Havana I shall have no one to care about me, and it will soon be over."

The man stopped abruptly.

"I am through," he said.

"You say you have no one to care for you," said the girl. "I will care for you."

But the officer only shook his head.

"I should ruin your hopes," he said. "You must not think of me at all. If I came I should have no way of taking care of you; I will stay in Cuba. And remember that I have done this to make you happy—because I love you. If I leave you unhappy I shall know that I have died for nothing."

And there the matter ended. The calm officer only shook his head to all of Bessie's arguments; he had his mind made up, and was as firm as adamant.

It seemed strange that the girl should be trying to persuade him to marry her; but in her earnestness she never thought of that. The man's sacrifice quite appalled her; she felt that she was not worth it, and she did all she could to persuade him of her sincerity.

But Lieutenant Hernandez was unmoved.

"I know that you love him," he said, "and I know that your heart is ready to break at the thought of leaving him. I can see it in the way you look at him. I knew it when you fainted when I spoke of his danger. And I do not blame you, for he is a braver man than I. But I will not be coward enough to separate you. You would hate me."

"Hate you?"

"Yes, and every decent American, too. What else has any man for a traitor? I should kill myself for shame. No, no!"

And the girl realized to her despair what he said was true; but oh! how her heart went out to that man!

The officer rose to his feet just then, as if to close the painful discussion. Bessie Stuart rose, too, and she held out her hand to him.

He took and kissed it reverently; then his face still calm and dignified, he stepped to the door.

"It is best," he said, "that I should go."

"Can you not wait to see us start?" asked the girl.

"You will find a boat on the shore just in front of you," began the other. "And you had best start as soon as it is light. But there is nobody about here, and you are not in any danger. As to my staying, I will watch you from the woods, a short ways back. It would not be well for me to stay here, for I am human——"

The man paused a moment as he gazed into the girl's beautiful face.

"I am very weak," he said, with a sad smile. "I might accept the reward you offer."

And with that he bowed, then turned resolutely on his heel and strode away into the darkness.

As he did so he passed Clif; and Clif, as he saw him leave rushed toward the dark figure that stood in the doorway of the hut.

What had been Clif's agony of mind may be imagined. When he saw the lieutenant going away it had flashed over him that perhaps he refused the act of treason implied in his going to America.

And Clif's heart began to throb once more with the wild hope he had tried so hard to suppress.

"Bessie!" he panted. "Bessie! What did he say?"

"He has gone back to Havana," was the answer.

For an instant the two stood staring at each other, their hearts throbbing with an emotion they were ashamed to call joy. Clif saw the girl's slender figure trembling.

And he sprang forward and caught her in his arms just as she fainted dead away.

CHAPTER XX.

AN UNEXPECTED PERIL.

How the long hours between then and sunrise passed away those two hardly knew. Bessie Stuart, exhausted by her long nervous strain, sank into a restless slumber. And Clif sat with his eyes fixed on the gradually lightening doorway.

Clif wanted to feel happy, but he scarcely dared. For he had before his mind the thought of that lonely Spanish officer, waiting somewhere in the distance to see them depart and leave him to his fate.

It was a solemn thought, and it made Clif tremble. He almost wished that the man had not rescued him.

But then again he thought of Ignacio and his frenzied cruelty, and he felt that he would have died himself to save any man from such a fate as that.

And now it was done and there was no undoing it. There was no way of aiding the lieutenant, no way of persuading him, nothing but death for him to face.

But as Clif sat there through the early hours of the morning and gazed upon that silent figure by his side he felt that his love for that girl was consecrated by that hero's sacrifice. There was a light of high purpose in the brave man's eyes; he was accepting his life and hers at the cost of another's, and the terms were such as made him feel the meaning of his existence. It was to be no child's play, no blind hunt for pleasure or wealth or fame, but a life with a purpose and meaning, a struggle for the right.

"I think his face will always be watching me," thought Clif.

And there were moments in his after life when the thought that that quiet Spaniard's eyes were watching made him shrink from the base things of life.

The light that shone in from the eastern sky gradually grew brighter and brighter, and Clif awakened from his solemn reverie to the duty that lay before him then.

He had Bessie Stuart to protect, and to lead from that position of peril.

It would indeed be a frightful calamity, he thought, if that sacrifice of Lieutenant Hernandez should avail nothing. If that girl should fall once more into the clutches of the Spaniards.

"For they are not all like that man," thought the lad.

And so he waited nervously until the light was bright enough. And then very gently he awakened her and assisted her to rise.

The girl was weak and exhausted, but she gathered her strength for this last final effort.

"We have not far to go," Clif said. "And we will soon be safe."

The two halted for a moment at the doorway of the hut and gazed out.

In the faint gray light they could not make out the line of the shore beyond, but they heard the noise of the breakers and knew that it was not far away.

And so half carrying his friend, Clif set out in the direction of the sound. Once only he turned again.

That was to take a parting look in the direction he knew Lieutenant Hernandez to be.

But he could make out only a dim line of woods behind him. No one could be seen, and the place was lonely and silent and gray.

But Clif fancied those quiet eyes were watching him from the distance.

There was no time to be lost, however, for no one knew when they might chance to meet with some of the enemy; they were in the midst of a thickly settled country.

And so they made their way swiftly down to the shore.

There they found a rowboat, drawn up on the beach a little beyond them. Clif was startled to see a figure standing by it.

But it proved to be only a boy, and he hailed them and then disappeared. Clif knew that he had been sent there to guard the boat; it was more of the lieutenant's thoughtfulness.

The sight of that guarantee of safety revived Bessie Stuart's spirits considerably; her step grew quicker and in a few moments they reached the spot.

There were a pair of oars in the boat, which was a small one. Without a word, Clif set to work to put it off from the shore.

That was as hard a task as could have been given him; for great waves were rolling upon the beach. But Clif was an athlete and a sailor besides; and the realization of their danger nerved his arm.

He seated the girl in the bow and ran the boat out with a rush; he caught a favorable moment. He plunged on until the water was up to his waist, and then he leaped into the boat and seized the oars just as another great wave swept them in toward shore again.

But Clif pulled for his life and held his own; and when the current set out again, he breasted the line of breakers and reached the sea beyond.

Bessie Stuart sat perfectly motionless, grasping the gunwale, until she saw that they were safe. Then she gave a slight gasp and closed her eyes wearily.

Clif had but one object, and that was to get as far from the coast of Cuba as he could; every stroke that he rowed put him further away from that dreaded shore.

And he knew, though he could not see them then, that far out to sea lay the vessels of the blockading squadron. Once in sight of them and the anxious fugitives were safe.

And so Clif put every ounce of muscle he had into that task. Not a word more was spoken; but the man's lips were set in a desperate resolve and his broad back heaved as he fought his way on.

There was a heavy sea, and progress was frightfully slow. Now that they were so near to safety, to be recaptured would be frightful indeed.

But yet the cadet knew that Spanish soldiers on the shore might catch sight of them at any moment, and come rushing down the beach to open fire.

Clif had rescued one man from just such a plight as that; and so as he rowed he glanced nervously along the shore.

But he saw no one, and no one saw him. The light brightened until he could make out everything along the coast, but there was no sign of any one's having noticed them.

An so with his heart growing lighter at every moment Clif tugged at the oars and forced the frail boat ahead through the waves. It was but natural that his relief should be great, for his adventures upon that island had been terrible ones indeed.

A warship is far from a safe place of residence, especially in war time. But Clif felt that if he once got under the American flag again all his worry would be at an end.

And so every stroke nearer was a cause for joy.

For perhaps five minutes he rowed on in silence. By that time he was some distance from shore, though their progress was slow in the heavy sea.

But they felt that they were safe. They felt that there was no longer anything to be feared. And there was a silent prayer of thanksgiving in Clif Faraday's heart.

And such being his feelings, the reader may imagine the horror and consternation that swept over him a moment later.

For an appalling discovery was made, one that seemed fairly to freeze Clif's blood.

He was struggling with his back toward Bessie Stuart. And the joy that was in his heart was turned to horror by hearing the girl give a shrill scream.

The cadet whirled about.

He saw the girl, her face transfixed and white as a sheet, pointing with a trembling finger off to starboard.

Clif followed the direction of her gaze; what he saw made his brain reel, made him almost totter backward into the boat.

Not half a mile away, coming straight down the coast and bearing down upon them at full speed, was a vessel, a low gunboat.

And high above her bow was floating a Spanish flag.

Clif stared at the frightful apparition as if he had seen a ghost.

What it meant to him may be imagined—the failure of all their hopes—their capture and death!

And there was not the slightest possibility of escape!

Perfectly wild with terror the agonized cadet whirled about, gazing seaward, with a faint hope of the possibility of there being seen by some American vessel.

But the gray horizon was not light enough for them to be sighted. And all hope was gone.

Bessie Stuart continued pointing to the vessel as if she were paralyzed by fright.

"Row! Row!" she shrieked.

And Clif seized the oars frantically. But he knew that it was utterly useless. The gunboat was coming on like a race horse.

And scarcely had he taken two strokes before the matter was settled finally. For there came a puff of white smoke from the Spaniard's bow.

And almost at the same instant with a deafening, blinding crash, a solid shot struck the tiny rowboat.

It plunged through, almost tearing the frail craft in half, hurling splinters about and sending the two horrified occupants tumbling into the water!

CHAPTER XXI.

RECAPTURED BY THE ENEMY.

Clif was so heartbroken at that sudden ending of all his hopes, that he scarcely cared whether he was drowned or not. But he saw Bessie Stuart struggling in the seething waters, and toward her he struck out desperately.

It took the cadet but a moment to reach her side. The shattered wreck of the wooden boat was floating near, and to that he struggled, helping her on.

And they reached it, in what it sounds like mockery to call safety. The girl scarcely knew whether it were best to hold on or to drown.

But instinctively she clung to the side as the great waves swept over them; and the two fixed their eyes upon the approaching vessel.

She came on swiftly, sheering the water with her sharp bow. And Clif could see half a dozen men standing in the bow watching them.

"Perhaps they have heard of our escape," he growled, "and come after us."

The vessel was not coming from Havana, but the cadet knew that a telegram might have sent it out.

At any rate, they were recaptured; and the horrors of Morro were before them again.

Steadily the gunboat drew nearer; the two half-drowned Americans were reached in a minute or two.

And the vessel slowed up and a rope was thrown to them. Clif desperate from despair, seized it and drew himself close.

A couple of Spanish sailors leaned down from the low side and lifted first the half unconscious girl and then the cadet up to the deck.

And then, weak and pale and dripping wet, they confronted a tall, ugly-looking Spaniard with an officer's chevrons.

He stared at them curiously.

"Who are you?" he demanded.

And Clif, grim with desperation, looked him in the eye and answered boldly:

"We are Americans," said he.

"Prisoners?"

"Yes."

"From where?"

"Morro Castle."

The Spaniard looked the amazement he felt.

"Morro Castle!" he echoed. "Humph! How did you get out?"

"Take us back there and you'll find out," was Clif's defiant answer.

And with that he turned toward the girl to wipe her dripping hair from her face.

He expected that the man would continue questioning them. But he was mistaken. The Spanish gunboat had done a risky thing, running out as it had, and her officers were anxious to get back.

The man turned away and hurried off. A sailor with a pair of handcuffs approached Clif, and the cadet quietly allowed his wrists to be secured.

Bessie Stuart was fortunately spared that indignity. The sailor gruffly ordered them to go below.

The vessel, meanwhile, had resumed her trip. She had been running along close to the coast under cover of the darkness of the previous night. And now she turned to steal back.

Clif's heart was heavy, and he was miserable beyond description.

But he turned and silently followed the sailor to the companionway.

They did not go below at once, however, for just then something occurred that made the sailor stop.

The man who had first spoke to Clif, the captain, apparently, had been sweeping the shore with his glass. And just then he gave a startled exclamation.

Everybody heard him, and the Spanish sailor stopped and turned to look.

Clif was so listless and despairing that he did not take the trouble to do likewise; but when he heard the exclamations of the men he felt his heart give a leap.

They were staring at a man on the shore.

"What in the world can be the matter with that fellow?" cried the captain.

"Santa Maria! he is calling to us!" exclaimed another.

"He must be crazy," declared a third.

The captain, with his glass could see more plainly than the others, and his astonishment grew greater.

"Why, he's a Spanish officer—a lieutenant, I think! And he is trying to hail us. What can it mean?"

"Perhaps he's got dispatches!" suggested some one.

It flashed over Clif in an instant what that meant, and Bessie Stuart heard him give a muffled exclamation of delight.

For he could see a blue-uniformed figure running down the shore and waving its arms wildly.

"It's Lieutenant Hernandez!" he panted.

And there was a wild gleam of hope in his eyes as he realized what that meant.

He might rescue them again!

Feverishly Clif watched to see what the gunboat would do. The captain continued staring and muttering exclamations of astonishment.

"I wonder if he does want us," he cried. "Por dios, I do think that's it."

And a second later he made up his mind and whirled about.

"Hard a port!" he roared.

And Clif's heart leaped with joy as he heard that order.

The sailor was so much interested in that strange incident that he let his prisoners remain on deck while he stood and stared. The Spanish vessel raced swiftly in toward shore.

And the stranger as soon as he saw that stopped his frantic gesticulating and stood still to wait.

The captain ran in as close as he dared, and then stopped. He stepped into the bow.

"What do you want?" he roared.

"Send a boat," the man shouted back. "I must come aboard. Quick!"

The captain muttered an exclamation of astonishment under his breath; but his curiosity alone would have been sufficient to move him. The gunboat's wherry boat was quickly gotten away.

As for Clif, he was simply wild with delight. For he could see that it was Lieutenant Hernandez after all.

Bessie Stuart was so overcome by the sudden shock of the discovery that she was scarcely able to stand, breathlessly the two watched the rowboat speeding in.

The lieutenant waded out as far as he could, and when the boat reached him he climbed into the bow. In a few moments he was speeding back to the gunboat.

And when he stepped on board he found the captain staring at him.

"Lieutenant Hernandez!" he gasped.

"Yes," said the other with a bow.

But he scarcely glanced at the man until his eager eyes had sought out Clif and Bessie. When he saw them alive and unhurt a look of relief swept over his face.

And then he turned to the captain.

"What in the world is the matter?" the man cried.

The other nodded toward the two Americans.

"It is about them," he said.

"What about them?"

"Why did you stop them?"

"Stop them! Why they are Americans, and they were prisoners in Morro."

"I know that," said the officer. "But they were released."

"What!"

"Yes. And I was charged with the duty of seeing them safe on board the American ships."

The Spanish captain stared in amazement.

"Carramba!" he muttered. "Why didn't they say so?"

"I don't see that you gave them a chance," said the other. "You fired on them too soon."

"But I had no idea of this!" cried the other.

To doubt that story never once entered his head; he seemed to know who the lieutenant was.

"What in the world am I to do?" he asked, after a moment.

"I don't see that there is but one thing," said the other.

"Take them back to Havana and let them be sent from there?" asked the captain.

"No," said the lieutenant, quietly. "That will not do; for the government has pledged its word that they shall be on the ships by daybreak. To make haste is very important."

"But what else?"

"Give them your small boat."

"Carramba! I haven't got but one! And how will I ever get it back?"

The lieutenant was puzzled for a moment.

But suddenly he hit on a daring scheme.

"Captain," he said, "my orders are from General Blanco himself. He charged me above all things to see these people safe at once, even if I had to go out to the ships with them. I don't see that there is but one thing we can do."

"What is it?"

"We will have to hoist a flag of truce and take them out on this vessel."

The captain started.

"Can we trust the Americans?" he gasped.

"They are expecting us," said the lieutenant quietly.

And then for a minute the captain was silent; when he spoke it was to the man at the wheel.

"Steer us out to the Yankee fleet," he said. "It will have to be done, and run up that white flag."

Perhaps ten minutes after that the blockading squadron sighted a Spanish gunboat coming toward them with a flag of truce.

The New York steamed to meet it; and the vessel came alongside and without a word of explanation the two prisoners were sent aboard.

Clif and Bessie both gazed longingly at the noble-hearted lieutenant as he stood on the deck and watched them leave. Their look said plainer than words, "Come with us!"

But he only shook his head; and when he saw the two disappear upon the deck of the big cruiser, and when the gunboat was well on her way back to shore he turned with a slight groan and went below.

Clif and Bessie wondered with anxiety and sorrow what would be his fate. They dreaded for him the worst tortures of Castle Morro, but the heroic Spaniard escaped that—in a way that Clif learned a few days later.

CHAPTER XXII.

CUTTING A CABLE.

The cadet's report was soon made. Under ordinary circumstances he would have been ordered to report back to the Uncas, but that stanch little gunboat was then miles beyond the western horizon. Moreover, the admiral had other work for the cadet.

As to Miss Stuart; there was a parting between her and Clif that was such as should be between acknowledged lovers, but it was a parting of the most decided kind, for his duty lay in the war, hers on land. She was sent to Key West on a cruiser that was then leaving the squadron to recoal.

What the young man and the girl said to each other cannot concern us here, for we have now to do with Faraday's experience as a sailor. His love affair had to await the events of war, and so may the story of it.

Clif's next service began on the morning following his escape. A small boat left the flagship and headed for Point Rubalcava on the Cuban coast. It was bent upon a dangerous mission; so hazardous, in fact, that volunteers had been called for to man the boat.

The first one to offer his services had been Clif Faraday. There was no lack of followers among the brave American tars. Fifty offered themselves a moment after the cadet stepped forward, and the task was to select from them twelve men to form the boat's crew.

"It is necessary to cut the cable as a war measure," said Rear Admiral Sampson, when the selection had been made. "You will proceed cautiously toward shore and grapple for the cable. If you find it, cut it. If not, you must go ashore and locate the landing place of the wire. Are you ready for the service?"

"Ay, ay, sir!" came the ready response.

Rear Admiral Sampson looked upon the brave, eager faces of the men for a moment with evident satisfaction.

"There is danger of discovery, and attack from the shore batteries," he added. "Success will depend upon your quickness and skill."

The men well knew the danger that lay before them, but there was no sign of faltering upon their faces. Rather, there was an eagerness for instant action that was not lost upon the commanding officer.

"Then go!" he exclaimed, heartily.

The boat was lowered, and quietly set out upon its mission.

It was in charge of a lieutenant, and Clif Faraday, in recognition of his being the first to volunteer, was placed beside him in the stern to steer the boat through the rough waters.

It was still dark, though the eastern sky gave promise of the near approach of day. The time had been selected to enable the boat to near the shore without great danger of detection in the dim light. But by the time they should succeed in grappling the cable there would be sufficient light to enable them to complete their task.

"All seems quiet on shore," said Clif, after a time, to the lieutenant, as they both peered forward at the coast line now looming up before them. "The Spaniards don't seem to be looking for us."

"True," responded the lieutenant. "It looks that way. But you can't sometimes always tell. They may have a surprise for us."

"If they don't shoot any straighter than they have been doing," said Clif with a laugh, "they'll never touch us."

"That's true, too," assented the lieutenant. "But still you must remember——"

"The Maine!" interrupted Clif.

"Yes, remember the Maine! But, as I was saying, these fellows might possibly aim at something else beside our boat and hit us accidentally. At any rate, I hope they don't see us. We are not out to capture a fort armed as we are with nothing but revolvers, and in this open boat we would be an easy prey to decent marksmanship."

"Still, the boys like action," said Clif.

"We may have plenty of it yet," replied the lieutenant, with a suspicion of uneasiness in his tone.

Meanwhile the boat, guided by Clif's hand, had drawn nearer the shore. They could see plainly the outlines of the fortifications, which had been recently battered by shell from American gunboats, and which they knew the Spaniards had attempted to repair. But as far as they could see all was quiet there.

The boat was following what was supposed to be the course of the cable, and the men were constantly seeking to secure it with their grappling irons. The crew proceeded cautiously but expeditiously with its work, the boat passing to and fro across what they supposed was the line of the cable.

"How is it, Wilson?" at last said the lieutenant, speaking to one of the men who was leaning over the side of the boat. "Struck anything yet?"

"Not yet, sir," was the response.

Nearer and nearer to the shore came the boat, the men coolly continuing their labors, seemingly as unmindful of danger as though the coast was not lined by hostile forces. The sun peeped above the face of the water to the eastward, and the darkness slowly receded before it. Every detail of the frowning fortification ashore was now plainly visible to the boat's crew.

Clif looked intently along the shore, but there was no hostile movement to be seen. But he realized that the fast growing light of the rising sun must betray their presence to the enemy, if any such were on watch.

"What a fine target we would make for them, too," he thought. "And close range at that."

His thoughts were interrupted by an exclamation from one of the men who had been previously addressed by the lieutenant.

"Hurrah!" cried the man. "I've got it!"

The boat was quickly brought to a standstill, and willing hands assisted him. In a few moments the heavy cable appeared above the surface of the water and was drawn up to the boat.

"Now, men, quick with the saws!" cried the lieutenant, excitedly. "Quick work, and we'll be done and away before the Spaniards discover us!"

It required quick work, indeed—quicker than any of the brave boat's crew then thought.

The lieutenant had no more than given his orders when an interruption, startling and unwelcome, occurred. He had been anxiously scanning the outlines of the fortifications and congratulated himself that no movement was visible in that quarter. The Spaniards were napping, he thought, and all was well.

But the reverse was the case, as he quickly discovered. No sooner had one of the sailors began to saw away at the cable than suddenly and without warning a shower of bullets rained around them in the water and the ominous boom of a cannon from the shore told they had been discovered.

"A masked battery to the left!" cried Clif. "They have ambushed us!"

This was true. The fortifications which had alone received the lieutenant's attention remained silent, while from the left a concealed battery kept up a raking fire upon the small boat and the intrepid crew.

The Spaniards had not yet gotten the range, it is true, but it was a tight place to be in—in an open boat, unarmed, helpless and exposed to the raking fire from shore.

But the men in that boat were full of nerve. Not once did they falter while shells and shot whistled and burst over their heads, beyond them and even among them.

"Hurry up, Wilson," cried the lieutenant to the sailor sawing the cable. "That cable must be cut before we leave the spot."

"Ay, ay, sir," responded the other. "If it kills every man of us!"

It began to look as if that would be their fate. The Spanish shot and shell, which at first fell harmlessly into the water, now dropped nearer and nearer. Clif heard an awful buzzing and whizzing sound in the air, and seemed to feel something hit him in the face and head. It was not his first time under fire, and he knew that a shell had passed near them.

The fire from shore increased in rapidity and with more accuracy. From another quarter, a jut of land nearer to the boat, came a fusilade from Mauser rifles, and their bullets passed near the heads of the American crew.

It was a hot place, but the men worked coolly on, determined that their orders should be executed at all hazards. By rapid work one piece of the cable was cut, but that was not enough. Another cut must be made at least fifty feet away, so that the Spaniards could not repair it by splicing. As the last strands parted and the free end of the cable fell back into the water, it was discovered that the sailor held the shore end in his grasp, and that to complete their work they must now draw closer to the fire of their enemies.

"Fifty feet nearer shore!" exclaimed the lieutenant, and the crew grasped the oars and unflinchingly began to carry out the order.

The shots of the Spaniards began to tell. Bullets splintered the sides of the boat, and they had not moved but a few feet from the spot when another volley severely wounded two of the men.

Wilson, the man who had been so active, fell into the bottom of the boat severely wounded in the shoulder, and another sailor who was near where Clif sat, was shot in the thigh. But the boat kept on, rowing nearer and nearer.

Clif resigned the tiller to the lieutenant, while he bound up the men's wounds and comforted them as best he could. Then he jumped back to the tiller.

This was an unfortunate move for him, for in that position he and the lieutenant were the most conspicuous figures in the boat, and the Spanish riflemen were making every effort to pick off the officer. A bullet, intended for the lieutenant, struck Clif in the arm as he took his place.

"Are you wounded?" shouted the officer above the din, noticing that Clif momentarily paled.

"It is nothing," replied Clif, resolutely clinching his teeth and continuing to guide the boat.

Just then the welcome sound of the firing of cannon to seaward reached their ears.

"It is the New York!" cried Clif. "She is taking a hand in the scrimmage!"

It was true. With deadly accuracy, the flagship was hurling shrapnel shell over the heads of the bluejackets into the battery on shore.

And thus between the two fires the little band in their frail boat continued coolly with their labors, Clif assisting those who became wounded wholly unmindful of the fact that he himself was bleeding freely.

But it was soon over. The terrible havoc of the well-directed shrapnel shot from the New York quickly silenced the masked battery and dispersed the gunners and the cutting of the cable received no further interruption from the Spanish forces.

They were enthusiastically received upon their return to the flagship, bearing a section of the cable to be cut up as souvenirs. The wounded were tenderly cared for, and Clif himself examined the nature of his own injury. Fortunately, though it had bled freely, it was but a slight flesh wound, which gave him no uneasiness after being properly bandaged.

This operation was just completed, when a jaunty young ensign appeared, and turning to Clif, said:

"Cadet Faraday, you are requested to report to the rear admiral at once."

Clif saluted and promptly followed the officer.

CHAPTER XXIII.

A PERILOUS DETAIL.

Clif did not have long to speculate upon the cause of the summons. The ensign led the way to the rear admiral's cabin, knocked, and with Clif closely following, entered. He then saluted and went out again, leaving the cadet alone with the officer.

Rear Admiral Sampson noticed the paleness of Clif's face, and thoughtfully directed him to sit down.

"I hear that you were wounded while cutting the cable," he said at once. "You were under hot fire while it lasted, and I am proud of the way the men behaved. I am told that you did not give up the tiller in spite of your injuries."

Clif, though pleased to receive the praise of the rear admiral, bore himself modestly. It did not seem to him that he had done any brave act.

"My wound was slight, sir," he said quickly. "It has been properly dressed, and gives me no trouble."

"I am glad to hear that," replied the officer, "for I have an especial mission upon which I desire to send you, but of course would not think of your going if it should endanger your health. Other danger you do not seem to fear."

Clif reassured the officer that he was ready and able to undertake any mission intrusted to him.

"It is briefly this," continued the rear admiral. "While you were out with the boat, I received a communication by the dispatch boat saying that a courier from the Cuban chief, Gomez, is to be at a certain spot near, the coast to-night, bearing important dispatches from the insurgents. It is necessary that we send some one to meet him, and your previous experience on Cuban soil and your knowledge of the Spanish language recommend you as the leader of the party. Are you prepared to go? There may be danger——"

Clif eagerly interrupted him. To his mind it seemed a great honor, as it really was to be placed in command of so important a mission, and he counted no danger great enough to cause him to hesitate.

He told the rear admiral as much, forgetting in his eagerness for active service, that he was but a cadet.

"Then it is settled," said the rear admiral. "To-night the New York will reach a spot nearly opposite the place of meeting, and you will be ready with a party of ten, whom you may select. Here is a diagram of that part of the coast, indicating the appointed spot where the courier is to be met."

He handed Clif a roughly drawn map, which the latter examined curiously.

"I know the spot well," he exclaimed, after looking at the diagram for a moment.

"All the better," said the rear admiral.

Then after some further directions and instructions from the officer, Clif saluted and took his leave, happy in the thought that he had been singled out for such important duty and that he would have this opportunity of active work.

He was really glad, though he would hardly admit it to himself, to be permitted to seek some rest during the day, for his wound was painful, if not serious.

It was late at night when, with a picked company of ten men, all armed, Clif parted company with the flagship and steered his boat toward the shore. The New York had dropped them near the appointed spot, but it had been deemed prudent not to take the ship near enough to attract attention to the intended destination of Clif and his crew. They therefore had considerable distance yet to row before touching land.

"I know the coast pretty well along here," thought Clif, as he set in the stern, tiller ropes in hand. "We'll get there all right."

Success depended upon their own efforts, for the New York slowly steamed away along the coast and in the opposite direction.

Clif and his party sped along without any uneasiness. It was night and darkness favored them. There was no reason to think that their presence there was suspected or their purpose known.

Still, for all this evident security, Clif kept a sharp lookout for any of the enemy who might be prowling along like himself, or, worse still, who might be scouring those waters with one of those silent little terrors, a torpedo boat.

All went peacefully until they were within less than half a mile of their destination, and quite near shore. Then suddenly a rifle shot rang out upon the shore, and sounds of voices came to their ears.

The Spaniards had discovered them!

"Perhaps not," thought Clif, hopefully. "Silence everybody," he said, addressing the men, "and listen."

Instantly the men ceased rowing, and every one strained his ears to hear the sounds from shore.

That there was a company of the enemy at that point was evident, from the noise of many voices and the confused sounds that were borne to the listeners' ears.

"They have discovered us," whispered Clif to the one nearest him. "I caught a few words of Spanish that convinces me that the sentry has heard our oars. Not a sound now! They can't see us in the dark, and will think it all a mistake."

It was a waiting game that Clif had set out to play, and it seemed the only thing that could help them under the circumstances. It was out of the question to think of attacking the Spaniards, superior at least in numbers. There was other work for the night.

Silently the American crew waited, listening for every sound. Soon these voices died out, and Clif concluded that they could venture to move once more.

"Row quietly," was his whispered order. "I'd like to give them a volley, but that would spoil our plans."

The men cautiously plied the oars and were soon steering softly toward their appointed place of landing. But quietly as they moved, the sound was borne ashore and they had not proceeded many boat lengths before another shot echoed across the water.

"To thunder with the Spaniard," exclaimed Clif, out of patience with the fresh outbreak. "He's firing at random. Go ahead. We'll meet them further down the shore if they're not satisfied."

This sentiment met the approval of the men, and they bent to the oars with vigor and spirit.

They were gliding swiftly across the water, and had nearly reached their landing place, when Clif heard a noise that put him on the alert.

"Do you hear that?" he exclaimed, after hastily stopping the rowers.

The men rested on their oars and listened.

"Sounds like the throbbing of an engine, sir," at last said one of the men. "It's a boat, sure."

"Yes, but friend or foe?" exclaimed Clif. "It's not the New York. She went in the other direction, and I don't know of any more of our boats in this place."

"Perhaps the New York is coming back," ventured one of the men.

"No," replied Clif. "She's not been here for at least three hours. By that time we will be ready to return to her."

"It must be a blockade runner," suggested one of the men.

"Well, I don't see as it makes any difference," said Clif, finally. "If it is, we can't stop her. She can't be after us, for I am sure no one of the enemy knows our mission. There is our landing place. We must hurry or we will be late."

With this he turned the prow of the boat toward shore, and gave orders to proceed. A few minutes later the boat grated upon the beach and the sailors sprang ashore.

There was no one to dispute their landing. The coast at this point was wild and uninhabited, and but a short distance inland was the spot appointed for the meeting with the insurgent courier.

Clif hid the boat among some bushes and quickly led the men up the steep bank toward a clump of trees.

"This is the spot," he exclaimed as they reached it, "and we are evidently ahead of time."

No one was in sight, as far as the eye could penetrate the darkness. There was barely enough light from the moon just emerging from behind a cloud to enable the sailors to take some notice of the surroundings. Where they stood, near the sparse clump of trees, it was smooth and level, but close to one side of them rose a ridge of ground forming a natural rampart. It almost seemed as though Spanish forms might at any instant appear upon it behind threatening guns.

Seaward the view was unobstructed, and as Clif turned his gaze in that direction, he could see the moonbeams reflected on the heaving bosom of the waters. He saw another sight an instant after that caused him to utter an exclamation of surprise.

Far out to seaward the beam of a searchlight suddenly shot across the water. It swept from side to side in a gradually widening radius, until after a few moments its glare fell upon a steamer whose hulk rose up between it and the shore.

"It is one of our ships chasing a blockade runner," cried Clif. "She was trying to sneak out, but is caught in the act."

The little party on shore watched with eager eyes the chase as shown by the bright beam from the warship's searchlight. In the excitement of the novel sight that was afforded them they for the moment forgot why they were there.

Then a strange and mysterious thing happened. As they watched the pursued vessel they suddenly saw a flash from a gun on the side facing the land.

"What fools!" cried Clif. "Firing toward the land instead of at our ship. The fool Spaniards must be rattled worse than usual. That beats——"

He did not finish the sentence. As he spoke the shell fired from the ship crashed through the trees and landed almost at his feet. The fuse was burning and spluttering, and it seemed ready to explode on the instant, carrying death and destruction to the little party.

It was a perilous moment. Several of the men instinctively dodged and seemed on the point of running away.

Clif saw his peril in an instant and the only hope of averting it. Without a moment's hesitation he sprang forward and picked up the shell as it seemed about to burst. With a mighty effort he hurled the spluttering missile over the ridge of earth that he had noticed to one side, and then, with an involuntary sigh of relief, he instinctively huddled with the balance of the party in an expectant attitude, waiting for the explosion on the other side of the rampart.

CHAPTER XXIV.

THE CUBAN COURIER.

But the explosion never came.

The party waited breathlessly, expecting to hear a deafening sound from the shell, and to see the earth thrown up in showers about them. From a safe place of vantage they felt it was a sight worth seeing and felt personally aggrieved when, after waiting an unconscionable time, all was quiet on the other side of the natural rampart of earth.

Clif had been surprised and puzzled in the first place to see the ship firing away from its antagonist instead of toward it, and was now more than ever perplexed. To add to the mystery, the ship did not fire another shot, either at its pursuer or in the opposite direction.

Its only purpose now seemed to be to get away from the American ship. It seemed to stand a good chance of doing it, too; for it was evidently a very swift boat, and the pursuing vessel was still far away.

"That's the queerest thing that ever happened," exclaimed Clif, when a sufficient time had elapsed to enable the shell to explode if it was ever going to. "What possessed them to fire over here, and what's the matter with the shell? I'll investigate the latter, at any rate; it's within easy reach."

Though it seemed as though more than enough time had passed to give the shell a good opportunity, still Clif, for reasons of prudence, concluded not to be too exacting on the thing, but to give it a fair chance. He didn't want to crowd it too close.

So he waited a while longer, and then cautiously climbed up the side of the embankment and peered over.

There in the moonlight he could see the shell lying quietly upon the ground. There was no smoke now rising from it, and the fuse had evidently burned itself out. It seemed a harmless enough piece of steel now.

He waited but an instant, and then vaulted over on the other side. His curiosity had been aroused regarding the matter and he for the time being lost all interest in the chase at sea, as well as the appointed meeting under those trees on shore.

When he picked up the shell he was more surprised and mystified than ever.

"What does this mean?" he exclaimed aloud. "A round shell of the old-fashioned type instead of the conical ones used nowadays! Why, a shell like this has not been used in any navy for ages!"

He had been too excited at the moment of picking up the spluttering shell to note its shape or size, but now he saw at a glance that the one he held in his hand was obsolete and out of date. It was well enough for the old-fashioned smooth-bore guns, but those of modern make had no use for them.

As he puzzled over the mystery surrounding the projectile he suddenly heard a whistle from the other side of the embankment. He recognized it as the signal from the insurgent courier, and at once was alive to the importance of carrying out the instructions that had been given him.

He hastily dropped the shell upon the ground and sprang up and over the ridge of earth.

He gave an answering whistle and soon a form cautiously appeared from among some bushes not far away.

"Alto quien va?" called Clif before the newcomer had advanced a step.

This was the challenge, meaning, "Who goes there?"

The response came promptly:

"Cuba!"

This is the countersign of the insurgents, and Clif knew that it was the courier who had reached the appointed rendezvous.

He called out to him to advance, and in the moonlight appeared the figure of an insurgent soldier, a mambis, as he is called in that country, a figure with which American tars were to become more familiar as the war progressed.

His equipment was typical of the insurgent soldier. Beside a pair of linen trousers and a knitted woolen shirt, he wore a short blouse, called mambisa. This was a small shirt-like vest, with pockets front and back, opening at the belt, a handy way of carrying their cartridges devised by them through necessity during the previous ten-years war. A panama hat turned up in front and fastened with a silver star, completed his attire; for as to his feet, they were innocent of a covering.

"Rather a summery outfit," thought Clif as he took it in with a glance.

But he knew that it was sufficient for the needs of the insurgents in that climate, and that brave hearts beat under the unpretentious mambisa, and brave deeds were done by the poorly equipped soldiers of the army of liberation.

The newcomer was effusive in his greeting.

"I bring you greeting from our brave general, Gomez," he exclaimed in Spanish. "Greetings to our noble friends and allies."

Clif received him cordially, but lost little time in preliminaries. Much more time had already been consumed than he had calculated upon, and he was anxious to have his business over with and return to the flagship with the important dispatches for which he had come.

"I am honored by your words," he said, in reply to the other. "Cuban liberty is assured by force of American arms, and at the same time we have our own score to settle with Spain."

"It will be done," said the Cuban.

"But to business," continued Clif. "You have some papers for me, have you not?"

"Yes," replied the courier, raising his blouse and drawing forth a package of papers from its place of concealment. "Important dispatches from our general for your gallant rear admiral. Besides much information concerning the Spanish fortifications and troops, there are details of our own plans and preparations which it would be ruinous to have fall into Spanish hands."

"I'll see that the Spanish don't get them," he said, with a confident air.

"Be cautious," exclaimed the Cuban. "The enemy have made one effort to intercept them. I was pursued a mile back from here, but my knowledge of the country enabled me to give them the slip. It was that encounter that delayed me."

This was a danger that had not been reckoned on. Every preparation for the transfer of the papers had been arranged with utmost secrecy.

"But did the Spaniards know of your mission here?" asked Clif, in some surprise.

"I know not," replied the other. "It is incredible how they could have discovered it, but I do know that I encountered a detachment of their troops and that they pursued me."

"Then they may be following you to this point," exclaimed Clif.

"I think not," replied the Cuban. "I made a wide detour and know the ways of the land too well to leave any trail."

"Nevertheless," said Clif, "our business is transacted, and the sooner we go our respective ways the better. These papers are now in my care, and I shall run no risk of their falling into the hands of our enemies."

"You are a wise officer," exclaimed the courier. "And before we part allow me to present you this. It may interest you."

With this he drew from his mambisa a paper which he quickly unfolded. It proved to be a sheet about ten by fourteen inches, and Clif could see, as he examined it by what light the moon afforded, that there was printing on both sides.

"This," said the courier, somewhat proudly, "is the first copy of 'Las Villas' ever printed. It is set up and printed at General Gomez's headquarters under his own direction. It contains, besides orders, and an address from our beloved general, an account of your intrepid Dewey's victory at Manila. Ah! that was a magnificent victory!"

"Yes," assented Clif, "and there will be others."

"The American battleships are invincible!" exclaimed the Cuban, with enthusiasm. "With such noble allies we cannot fail to secure our liberty. We are no longer instruments, but members of the regular army of Cuba. God bless America!"

The Cuban seemed in a fair way to continue his rhapsodies indefinitely, but Clif, having secured the papers for which he came, was now intent upon delivering them as soon as possible to the rear admiral.

He therefore intimated as much to the courier, and the latter took his departure.

Clif watched him disappear among the trees in the direction by which he had approached.

"Now, men," said he, addressing his companions, "to the boat. The New York will soon be back ready to receive us."

But they had not taken more than a few steps toward the shore when Clif suddenly stopped as if remembering something.

"Hold on just a minute!" he exclaimed. "That shell! I have special reasons for wanting to carry that along. It will take but a minute to find it."

As he started toward the ridge of earth beyond which he had thrown it, they were all startled to hear the sounds of musketry apparently near at hand. One volley was quickly followed by another.

Clif sprang upon the embankment for which he had started, and looked off beyond the clump of trees in the direction from which the sounds came.

He was in that position but a moment or two. A half-dozen reports in quick succession greeted his appearance—one bullet passing through his cap.

He dropped on his feet to the ground beside his companions.

"The Spaniards!" he exclaimed, hurriedly. "At least a hundred of them. From what I saw they were hurrying in this direction and not far away."

They were on the alert on the instant. The sounds that reached their ears told them unmistakably that the force of the enemy far outnumbered their own, and were rapidly approaching.

Should they await an attack or run for the boat?

CHAPTER XXV.

"IN THE NAME OF HUMANITY AND THE SAILORS OF THE MAINE!"

"They must have followed the courier in spite of his cleverness," exclaimed Clif. "And if they have tracked him, they know we are here. The question is, shall we meet them here or take to the boat and run the risk of being shot down without a chance to defend ourselves? The danger is yours as well as mine. What do you say?"

But before the men could make reply a rousing cheer from the Spanish soldiers rang out upon the air.

The little band of Americans expected to see the forms of their enemies appear among the trees at every second in an impetuous charge upon them. They had no doubt that the cheers were the signal for the attack.

But to their amazement the sounds of approaching steps died out. Clif's practiced ear told him that the enemy had halted; but at the same time he recognized marks of enthusiasm among the Spanish forces.

What could it mean?

"Do they think they can scare us off by yelling at us?" exclaimed Clif, contemptuously. "They don't know us, if they think so—that's all!"

The group of Americans listened intently. There was no doubt of it, the Spaniards had halted after their vociferous cheers.

Clif decided to find out what it meant. If the Spaniards were preparing a surprise for him, he intended finding it out.

Cautiously he climbed upon the little rampart of earth and looked away beyond the trees where he had first seen the approach of the enemy. In the moonlight he could plainly distinguish the forms of the soldiers. There were not as many as he had at first supposed—they numbered not more than fifty.

In the midst of them he recognized a figure that explained the cause of their mysterious conduct, and at the same time aroused his fighting instinct.

He quickly rejoined his companions, his eyes ablaze with the fire of combat.

"They have captured the courier," he explained to his waiting companions. "That was why they cheered so lustily. A lot of jubilation over the capture of one man!"

"They don't have such good luck very often," exclaimed one of the men.

"They fired enough shots to repulse a whole regiment of insurgents," exclaimed Clif, "but it was all for the benefit of this one mambesi. I don't believe they saw me at all, but that bullet through my cap was one of their stray shots."

"But they must know we are here," exclaimed the men.

"I doubt it," replied Clif, "else why do they halt so near and not charge on us? Shall we force the fight and go to the rescue of our Cuban friend?"

"How many are there of them?" asked one of the men.

"Only about fifty."

"And there are eleven of us here! We can set them on the run! Let's do it."

"We have done almost as much on other occasions," said Clif, "but now we are armed with only our revolvers. They are five to one."

"We have plenty of ammunition," spoke up the men, eagerly. "You know we took an extra supply."

"But there is another thing we must bear in mind," said Clif, who had been doing some quick thinking. "I'd like nothing better than to give them a lively tussle. But here are these important dispatches. They must not fall into Spanish hands. The New York will soon be due. If we delay we might miss her."

"That's so," exclaimed the men. "But we can fire one volley at them anyhow."

"One volley would do no good. It would simply betray our presence. Either we must fight to the end, or else sneak off to our boat before they discover us."

The idea of having a lot of the enemy so near at hand and not offering them battle, went against the grain of all of them. They were not deterred by the superior numbers of the Spaniards, but Clif's words about the importance of seeing the dispatches safely in the rear admiral's hand had some restraining effect upon their ardor.

Clif, with all his bravery, was naturally prudent, but was strongly tempted to make one effort to release the captive Cuban. He was their friend and ally, and in his heart Clif felt that if the captive were one of his own men, there would be no thought of hesitancy or delay.

"One minute," he said, after weighing both sides of the question, "I'll take a look and see what they are doing."

He sprang upon the embankment and peered off toward the enemy. The main body of the troops were resting on their arms, apparently satisfied with the capture of the solitary Cuban.

Clif, however, could see that several of the soldiers were moving about from side to side, close to the ground, as though hunting for some object among the grass. Clif was puzzled to think what they could be seeking, but he felt convinced that the Spaniards had no idea of the near proximity of the Americans.

Everything seemed to prove that, and Clif was not slow to make up his mind. There was time yet for some quick action.

"They don't know we are here, men," he exclaimed, when he rejoined the others. "The Cuban will not betray us. We can surprise them, and if we sweep down on them with a rush and create noise enough about it we can make them think the whole ship's crew is after them."

"We'll do it!" chorused the men, eagerly.

"Then, forward to the rescue!" cried Clif, leading the way. "But quietly through these trees until we reach the other side."

It would seem a foolhardy thing to do—to invite battle with such an overwhelming force, when they might quietly reach their boat and make away without detection. But their blood was up, and there was a friend and ally in peril of a Spanish dungeon or death.

Without a moment's hesitation or further thought, they advanced silently through the sparse woods, revolvers in hand. They were few in numbers, but determination was written on every face.

They reached the further edge of the clump of trees without giving a sound that would betray their presence to the enemy. Here they formed in line under Clif's leadership, shoulder to shoulder, ready for the charge.

The moon had gone behind a cloud, but here and there they could detect the glistening of a hostile bayonet, and the sound of Spanish voices.

They did not pause to contemplate the scene. The time for action had come.

"The stars are fighting with us!" exclaimed Clif. "The Spaniards will never know how few we are in this darkness. Now, all together. A rousing cheer and at them!"

At the signal a shout as of a hundred voices startled the unsuspecting Spaniards.

"Fire!" cried Clif and a volley from their revolvers carried consternation into the Spanish ranks.

The shots had told. Groans of the wounded mingled with the hoarse, startled commands of the officers.

A moment later a return volley rang out upon the air, but the bullets flew harmlessly among the trees. The Spaniards in their fright were firing wildly.

The Americans returned the fire and kept it up as rapidly as possible, yelling for all they were worth. This noisy charge had the effect Clif had reckoned upon. The Spaniards were thoroughly frightened and Clif's sharp ear told him that some of the soldiers were already on the run, and that the officers had difficulty in keeping them all from retreating.

Clif knew very well that if the enemy had any idea of how meagre were his forces they would be bolder, and instead of trying to get away would sweep down upon him with overwhelming force. He, however, was too shrewd to give them a chance of finding that out. A bold dash would keep up his "bluff," and now was the time to put it into execution.

Drawing his sword, he started toward them, shouting at the top of his voice:

"Up and at 'em, boys!" he roared. "Charge!"

Then facing about for an instant, he added in a lower tone:

"Yell like sixty!"

With a wild shout, the little band rushed forward, firing their revolvers as they advanced in compact line.

This bold dash had the desired effect. The enemy could be heard retreating in disorder before them.

With redoubled clamor the Americans pressed forward, spurred on by the excitement of the chase. The moon at this point emerged from its retirement and showed them the demoralized ranks of the fleeing Spaniards.

But, unfortunately, it also showed to such of the enemy as looked back at their pursuers, what a handful of men had caused such terror and havoc. Clif felt that his "bluff" would now be called.

But the beams of the moon also showed another scene that aroused all the Americans' indignation and fairly made their blood boil with rage.

In spite of the panic the Spaniards had retained hold of their prisoner. But the first sight that Clif saw as the moon shone out clear once more, was one of the Spanish soldiers deliberately placing his revolver against the unfortunate Cuban's head and sent a bullet crashing into his brain.

"Treachery! base treachery!" cried Clif, beside himself with indignation and horror at the scene. "Assassination of a prisoner of war! Boys, shall we allow such a vile deed to go unavenged?"

The others had also seen, and there was no need to ask the question. But the answer came prompt and without a dissenting voice:

"No, by thunder! Never!"

"Then at them to the death!" cried Clif, leading them on. "In the name of humanity and the sailors of the Maine!"

The blood-curdling atrocity had made demons of them all, and with a hoarse shout they sprang to the charge.

CHAPTER XXVI.

A GAME OF BLUFF.

Clif urged his little band of avengers forward with no thought of danger or of the consequences. The inhuman scene he had witnessed drove from his mind all thoughts of the flagship or the important papers he carried upon his person.

Such barbarity called for vengeance, and that brave American handful of American tars meant to wreak it on their treacherous foes, or die in the attempt.

"Come on!" shouted Clif, wildly. "Give it to 'em! Don't let a man escape!"

A well directed volley was the answer to his command, that sent death-dealing bullets among the frightened soldiers just before them. But, unfortunately for the heroic little band, they were now fighting in the open, and their strength was known to the enemy.

A little further ahead Clif could see that a Spanish officer had succeeded in rallying some of his men, and they were now forming in solid line to repulse the charge of the Americans.

The first result of this was a shower of bullets from the Spanish rifles that fortunately for the most part went wide of the mark. But one slightly wounded a sailor at Clif's side, as a sharp exclamation of pain quickly told him.

It also aroused his native caution. What was the use, he quickly thought, of holding his men there in the full glare of the moonlight as a target for the enemy's guns, when a more certain conflict could be carried on from the shelter of the trees just behind him? He had too few men to risk losing any on those uneven terms.

He quickly ordered his men to drop back into the woods. But it was with great difficulty at first that he could inforce his commands upon the now thoroughly aroused sailors. They wanted to continue their impetuous charge.

But a second volley from the remaining troops showed them the wisdom of Clif's decision, and with a return volley they fell back into the darkness and shelter of the trees.

"Now, boys," cried Clif, "every man behind a tree and fight for all you are worth. Let every shot tell."

The wisdom of Clif's stand became at once apparent. From the ambush of the woods they could fire with little fear of stopping a Spanish bullet with their own bodies.

And they did fire, and that to good purpose.

The Spaniards were now bolder and bore down upon the ambushed Americans with some semblance of order. But at each volley from the sailors there was a wavering in the ranks of the foe, and Clif could see that more than one dropped wounded from the ranks.

"We'll lick 'em yet!" cried Clif, with enthusiasm. "Keep it up, boys!"

But the Spaniards advanced steadily in spite of their losses. They, too, were fully aroused at the thought that they had been so roughly handled by such a small number of men.

Clif and his gallant band were compelled to drop back from tree to tree. It began to look as though the Spaniards would in the end become victorious.

But with the Americans it was do or die. There was no hope of help or succor from any source. No reinforcements were at hand, and none could be sent in time from the flagship, even did those on board suspect the plight in which that boat's crew found itself.

But desperate cases require desperate measures, and Clif was equal to the emergency. When it became evident that the Spaniards would indeed fight, Clif's busy brain thought of a means to turn the tide of conflict.

It was a slight hope, to be sure, but the only one that presented itself. He smiled in spite of himself, in view of his meagre forces at the thought that the only way to achieve victory was by a flank movement.

"I'll take two men," he said hurriedly, "and slip around behind those fellows. The rest of you keep up your fire here, and if our lungs hold out we'll make them think we have reinforcements."

It was a very risky move, but with two companions Clif put it into execution at once. They hurried through the woods so as to flank the enemy, an easy task, as the latter were now well up to the little grove.

As they reached the edge of the woods which would bring them in the enemy's rear, they set up a mighty shout.

"At them, boys!" Clif yelled at his imaginary forces. "Come on! we've got 'em!"

Then in Spanish he cried, so that the enemy could hear:

"Surrender, you Spaniards! Twelve men have held you, and now we'll take you!"

He had reached the edge of the clearing, and paused a moment, facing around and beckoning to his imaginary reinforcements.

The Spaniards were completely bewildered. The fire from those that Clif had left behind continued without intermission, and the Spaniards could not but think that the vociferous sailors in their rear were new arrivals.

They could not in the first place conceive of the daring and hardihood that would lead a dozen men to oppose their forces unless reserves were near at hand. And now, thought they, these reinforcements had arrived.

Clif and his companions made noise enough to give color to this belief, and without stopping to see what there was behind the demonstration, the Spaniards took to their heels.

"They are not men, but devils!" Clif heard some one say in Spanish, as they dropped their rifles and start on the run.

Even the officer who had succeeded once in holding a remnant of his panic-stricken forces together, now gave up the fight and sprinted away as fast as the rest.

Every man seemed to be looking for his own safety, and they did not pause to see what was behind them. Here and there, it is true, one of the fleeing Spaniards could be seen helping a wounded companion in his flight. But as for further resistance, there was none.

Clif could not forbear to laugh at the odd sight of an army in a foot race to escape a few American sailors.

"American bluff has won the day," he laughed. "Our Cuban friend's death has been avenged, and that without the loss of a man on our side."

"The Spanish are good sprinters, at any rate," said one of the men, as they started with Clif to rejoin their companions.

Here Clif had all he could do to restrain his followers from continuing in pursuit of the enemy.

"No," said he in response to the earnest pleading. "We had better leave well enough alone. These Spaniards say we are not men, but devils, and I guess they don't care for another interview. The New York no doubt is waiting for us, and these dispatches are yet to be delivered."

There was no use to grumble, so the party set out on the return to their boat. They were highly enthusiastic over the good work done under Clif's leadership, and were proud of his pluck as well as the good generalship he had shown.

The tide of battle had carried them some distance from the spot where they had met the Cuban courier, and further still from where they had concealed their boat.

But they picked their way expeditiously through the woods, and reached the beach without further incident.

They were near the clump of trees which they recognized as that behind which they had hidden the boat when Clif stopped with a sudden exclamation.

"Gorry!" he said, "I have forgotten that shell. It won't take but a minute to return for it."

"What's the use, sir?" ventured one of the men. "As you said, we'd better let well enough alone, and not run any further risk for a shell that don't even explode."

"That's just the reason I want it," said Clif. "That shell is more important than you might think. I'll——"

But here occurred an interruption that opened up more startling possibilities, and drove the unexploded shell from the attention of all.

It was in the shape of an exclamation of surprise and alarm from one of the men who had gone a few steps in advance of the others, and had reached the boat's hiding-place as Clif spoke.

It arrested Clif's attention at once.

"What's the matter?" he called, sharply.

"The boat, sir," cried the marine, appearing from behind the bushes.

"What of it?"

"It's gone!"

"Gone?"

"Yes, sir."

Clif, followed by the others, hastened to the spot.

The man had spoken the truth. The boat, which now their sole dependence, was no longer there.

They looked in blank amazement at one another and at the spot where they had fastened it in fancied security.

What could it mean?

CHAPTER XXVII.

IN WHICH CLIF MEETS WITH A SURPRISE.

They were now in a perilous position.

They could not return to the flagship, and at any moment the Spaniards, finding they were not pursued, might pluck up courage to seek them out and try conclusions with them once more. If they should find them on that narrow strip of beach the story of the conflict might be a different one.

And then the disappearance of the boat itself pointed to enemies they had not counted upon. Who could have found and taken it?

"Well, now we're in a pretty pickle," exclaimed Clif, when he became satisfied that the boat had really been taken.

"Perhaps, sir, this is not the place where we left it," ventured one of the men, catching at that faint hope.

"I wish you were right," said Clif, "but there's no doubt about it. The boat has been taken."

"There's no doubt of it," the men echoed. "The boat is gone."

But to make assurance doubly sure, they searched the beach under Clif's direction, examining every clump of bushes that was large enough to conceal the boat. But the result was a foregone conclusion. The boat was gone.

"Now what's to be done, sir?" asked one of the men.

What, indeed!

"Something's got to be done," said Clif, with determination. "We've got to get off this island before daybreak. It's easy to dodge the Spaniards in the darkness, but entirely a different matter by day. Besides, we seem to have enemies down here as well as back there on the hill."

He was scanning the water earnestly as he spoke. It was time, he knew, for the flagship to return to her position opposite that point, and await the return of Clif and his crew.

Was she there?

He could not tell. The face of the moon was again obscured by clouds as it had been most of the night, and it was impossible for Clif to discern any object at a distance across the water.

He strained his eyes trying to catch a glimpse of the ship they had left not many hours ago, but the thought occurred to him, "What good will it do if I do see her?"

But even as he looked the sky suddenly brightened in a tiny spot out to sea. A long pencil of light shot up from the water, and a cloud was tinged with a speck of dull white light.

"It's the New York!" cried Clif. "The signal of her searchlight to return."

They watched that tiny beam of light as though there was hope of succor in its rays, until it suddenly disappeared, and all was dark as before.

"Now they are waiting for our appearance," said Clif. "But, unfortunately, we haven't got wings. Hello! What does that mean?"

Clif had turned suddenly in a listening attitude toward the land. The others had heard the same sound that had attracted Clif. It was the solitary report of a rifle shot not far in their rear.

"The Spaniards must be returning," said Clif. "They have made up their minds that we had no reinforcements because we did not pursue them further. I'll go up and reconnoitre, to see what they are up to."

"I'll go, sir," volunteered one of the men before Clif could get away.

"You stay here. You may be able to see some way of getting us off."

With this he cautiously hurried up the side of the bank, leaving Clif and his companions in the shelter of the bushes below.

With ears alert to any sound by land, they anxiously strained their eyes across the water. Could any way be found to cross the expanse that lay between them and the flagship?

All were silent for many minutes, and then at last the searchlight of the flagship flashed out once more and swept across the waters before it disappeared.

"So near and yet so far," exclaimed Clif. "They are getting impatient for our return."

"If we could signal them," suggested one of the men, "they would send a boat."

"But we have no means of doing that," said Clif. "We can't shout at them, and a pistol shot would not be heard, except by our friends the enemy."

"Perhaps they will send a boat anyhow," persisted the hopeful member of the crew.

"Perhaps," assented Clif, "after they get tired of waiting for us."

In a short time the scout returned with news that was at least disquieting in their situation.

"The Spaniards are after us, sir," he reported. "They seem to have rallied most of their men, and are now near the woods where we met them, cautiously advancing. They have scouts out looking for us, for I barely escaped running into one of them."

"They have guessed the trick we played on them," said Clif, "and it will go hard with us if they find us. How near are they, did you say?"

"They seem to be in the woods now, but they are advancing steadily. They are scouring the place thoroughly, and may be down on us any moment."

"Well, boys, we'll do the best we can, if they do get here," said Clif, quietly.

A calm settled upon the band, for now they knew their situation was critical. Their ammunition was nearly exhausted, and if the enemy should succeed in attacking them from the vantage of the hillside, there was little hope of a successful resistance. Should they succeed in eluding the enemy in the darkness, there was no doubt that daybreak would seal their fate.

"There's no two ways about it," exclaimed Clif. "We've got to get off this island, and that pretty soon."

"See, sir," cried the hopeful member, who had been intently gazing across the water. "They have sent a boat!"

Clif looked in the direction in which the other was eagerly pointing.

Sure enough, he could discern the outlines of a boat slowly moving toward them some little distance from shore.

An involuntary little cheer went up from the others as they, too, saw the boat approaching.

"We are saved!" exclaimed Clif, "and these dispatches will soon be in the rear admiral's hands."

But suddenly the eager watchers saw the boat stop, then after a few moments veer around, and continue its course down the coast until it was almost abreast of the spot where they stood.

Then it as suddenly stopped, and after a moment's pause retraced its course.

"What's the matter with those fellows?" exclaimed Clif. "Are they afraid to land?"

"Hadn't we better signal them, sir?" suggested the man. "They don't know where we are."

The boat had again turned and was apparently patroling up and down, seemingly waiting for just such assistance in locating the position of the waiting sailors.

But just as Clif was about to attract their attention by a mighty shout, his practiced ear caught sounds from the hill above that caused him to stop. The Spanish soldiers were unmistakably advancing.

"Silence!" he cautioned, in a whisper. "The Spaniards are on the hill above us and the slightest noise will betray us."

"But the boat, sir!" exclaimed the man. "We must signal it."

"I'll bring it here," said Clif, with a sudden resolve.

He began divesting himself of his blouse and trousers as he spoke.

"What do you mean to do, sir?" asked the men, wonderingly.

"Swim for it," replied Clif. "That's the only way."

"But, sir——"

"Don't delay me," said Clif. "Every moment is precious now."

With this he quietly slid into the water and with quick, powerful strokes shot through the waves toward the boat.

Clif was in his element.

In the whole ship's crew none excelled him in swimming and diving, and it was with a feeling of confidence that he forced his way through the water.

He made not a sound as he went along—for it was to avoid alarming the Spaniards that he had hit upon this plan.

The boat was not far from shore and he reached it in a few moments. He was overjoyed to recognize that it was, as he expected, one of the boats from the flagship.

There were two occupants of the boat, one at the oars and the other in the stern. Clif did not recognize them, but he did not pause on that account. Time was precious, and the boat must be gotten to shore and the balance of the party taken aboard without delay.

"Boat ahoy!" he exclaimed joyously, as he reached the side without having been seen by the occupants. "Take me aboard, men, and then pull for the shore for all you are worth."

Clif's sudden appearance and the words he spoke had a startling effect upon the oarsman by whose side Clif made his appearance.

The latter started with an oath, and as Clif seized the side of the boat and raised himself partly from the water, his gaze fell upon the glistening barrel of a revolver and back of it he saw a face distorted with rage and hate.

"Carramba!" fell upon Clif's ear. "It is an Americano! Death to the American pigs!"

The occupants of the boats were Spaniards.

CHAPTER XXVIII.

A STRUGGLE AGAINST ODDS.

The position in which Clif found himself was so startlingly unexpected and so full of peril that for a brief instant it almost unnerved him.

Had he suspected the possibility of the boat being manned by Spaniards, he would have given up the thought as soon as he recognized it as one belonging to the flagship. It seemed natural that a boat should be sent to look for them after their protracted absence, and it was a decided shock to find that he had fallen, alone and unarmed, in the way of his enemies.

But his surprise affected him but for an instant. He did not propose to be shot down if he could help it.

The report of the pistol that met Clif's gaze rang out upon the air, but the bullet did not reach its intended mark.

Like a flash Clif had released his hold upon the boat, and dropped beneath the water, just in the nick of time.

The Spaniard peered over the side of the boat in the darkness, expecting to see Clif's form appear on the surface, and hoping to see his life's blood staining the waters, a testimony to his marksmanship.

How could he have failed to send that bullet crashing through the American's brain? thought he.

But nothing of the sort happened. Clif not only was not wounded, but was chipper as a lark. When he disappeared, he dove under the boat and rose again on the opposite side. The Spaniard would look in vain in that spot for his intended victim.

But the Spaniard in the bow discovered Clif's head as it appeared for an instant above the water. With an imprecation of wrath he called his companion's attention to the spot. But one of them was armed, it seemed.

The other rushed to that side, but when he looked in the direction indicated, revolver in hand, Clif had again disappeared.

The American lad was as lively as a cricket, and busy thoughts surged through his brain.

In the first place, he did not propose being a target for a Spanish bullet. But, above all, he wanted that boat, and, like the cowboy when he wants a revolver, wanted it "bad."

"How can I get it?" he thought, as his dive brought him up near the bow of the boat. Help came from an unexpected source, for a few moments after, he was driven by a new peril to attempt the only plan that could accomplish it.

The agency that led to his delivery was a shark. That was not the every-day business of his shark-ship—that of saving an imperiled life for those inhabitating those waters are especially hungry and voracious.

But it happened this way: As Clif was quietly keeping himself afloat at the bow of the boat, confident that in that position he ran little risk of immediate discovery by his enemies, the plans and schemes revolving in his mind were brought to a sudden standstill by a sight that filled him with horror. A sharp triangular fin cutting the water like a knife, flashed past him.

"Merciful Heaven!" he muttered under his breath. "A shark!"

Death faced him on every side. To be sure he might frighten the shark by churning the surface of the water, but that very act would betray him to a no less certain death at the hands of his enemies.

His resolve, a desperate one that caused him to shudder as he formed it, was reached on the instant. The broad back of his enemy, who sat in the stern, was within easy reach, and inspired his action.

Quick as a flash Clif grasped the stern of the boat with one hand and with one mighty effort raised himself high out of the water. Before the Spaniard could divine what was happening, Clif's free arm was thrown around the fellow's neck, and he was drawn back into the water behind him.

An instant after Clif clambered over the stern into the boat. With a shudder at the thought of the fate that awaited the luckless Spaniard, he addressed himself to the work that lay before him.

And there was plenty of it, and lively, too, while it lasted.

The other Spaniard, who had been peering into the water ahead, turned sharply around when he heard the noise made by the splash of his companion, and in the act involuntarily dropped the revolver.

What must have been his feelings upon beholding the lithe and dripping form of the plucky young American emerging from the sea, may well be imagined.

But Clif did not pause to study the effects. He seized an oar and sprang toward his remaining foe.

"Surrender, you villain!" he cried in Spanish as he advanced.

The Spaniard seized an oar and with an oath sprang toward the American.

And there, on the quiet bosom of the water in the dim light of night, ensued a stubbornly contested duel, in which oars took the place of broadsword and sabre.

Clif fought savagely and desperately. His blood was up, and he knew that now, if ever, he was, fighting for his life.

But in the end it was fortune that favored him. A chance blow upon his antagonist's head rendered the latter unconscious, and victory again perched upon the young American's banner.

There was no time for exultation, even if he had felt that way. The work had been too serious, and necessity for action was too imperative.

Satisfied that he had nothing to fear from his enemy, now lying helpless in the bottom of the Boat, Clif seized the oars and turned the boat toward shore.

It was trying work for one man to row that boat even the short distance that lay between him and shore—especially after the ordeal through which he had passed. But excitement buoyed him up and he made good progress.

His companions in the shade of the bushes where he had left them had witnessed his exciting duel and were wrought up to tense excitement. How they bemoaned the fact that they were not there to help him!

It became evident that there were other spectators, too; for no sooner had Clif seized the oars and began to row for the shore than a volley of bullets rattled out across the water from the hill that had witnessed such thrilling scenes earlier in the night. The Spanish soldiers had discovered Clif!

In the face of this, Clif redoubled his efforts to reach the beach and rescue his companions, who might any moment be attacked by the soldiers in their rear.

But the enemy's attention was concentrated upon Clif and his boat, and he shot through the waters in a perfect hail of missiles. They spattered into the waters all around him, but wide of their mark.

He reached the shore, and as he sprang upon the ground his faithful little band could not repress a cheer at his bravery and pluck.

But he urged them on. Not a moment could now be lost. The enemy, shut off temporarily by the overhanging hill, might be down upon them any second.

Clif gathered up his clothing and at a word they all sprang to their places and the boat leaped through the water with a bound, and was away.

"To the flagship!" Clif cried, and then uttered an exclamation of alarm.

"The dispatches!" he cried, as he felt among his clothes. "They have been left behind!"

At a word the boat was turned round and shot swiftly toward the beach.

Yelling Spaniards could be heard racing down the hillside. They had discovered the landing-place, and bullets began again to rain about the water.

It seemed sure death to return in the face of that fire, but the intrepid crew sped on. The dispatches must not fall into Spanish hands!

The boat grated on the sands, and Clif sprang out. One instant brought him to the spot where his clothes had lain. Fortune favored him. As he felt along the ground, his hand touched a package of papers.

"The dispatches!" he cried, as he sprang to his place in the stern of the boat, which had been turned ready for the start. He gave the word and away they sped, this time with the flagship as the goal. Spanish bullets flew after them, but they were safe. It was only when they were for a moment brought out into bold relief by the searchlight that again began to play from the flagship that the bullets of the enemy came near their mark.

And then the firing ceased and the boat sped on. An enthusiastic and jubilant crew it was. Only Clif seemed in a dissatisfied mood.

"Gorry!" he suddenly exclaimed, "I came off without that shell after all!"

"You seem to lay great store by that, sir," said one of the men.

"I do," said Clif. "But will not return for it just now. To the flagship!"

Not many minutes later they were safe aboard, the captured Spaniard in proper custody, and, best of all, the dispatches were personally delivered by Clif to the rear admiral.

But still Clif was not entirely satisfied.

CHAPTER XXIX.

CLIF'S SECOND EXPEDITION.

In spite of the glorious work accomplished in those few hours Clif felt chagrined that he had, in the excitement of the struggle on the boat and under fire of the Spanish soldiers on shore, been forced to return to the flagship without the shell.

He had thought considerably about it even during the stirring scenes through which they had passed. He had his own ideas about it and wanted to put them to the test.

Everything connected with it indicated to his mind some mystery, the solution of which would materially help the American forces.

In the first place, the way in which it was brought to his attention was unusual, to say the least. That a ship being pursued by a hostile craft should deliberately fire away from the pursuer and toward the land was peculiar, even for a Spaniard.

It was ridiculous to think that the shell had been aimed at Clif and his party, for even had it been broad daylight the American boat's crew would not have been visible to those on the Spanish ship. It was merely a coincidence that Clif happened to be where the shell landed.

"No," thought Clif as he revolved this in his mind, "that shot was not aimed at our forces. There was some other reason for firing it."

What that was he could merely conjecture, and he was not entirely clear in his own mind. That the mysterious purpose had been carried out to the satisfaction of those on the Spanish boat, Clif felt convinced, was evident from the fact that not another shot was fired.

Then the shape of the shell was an important factor.

"They are not using those round ones nowadays," thought Clif. "This one must be used for a special purpose. What that is, I'm going to find out."

The arrival of the Spanish soldiers and their peculiar actions before the little battle that followed also demanded explanation.

"They didn't know we were there," mused Clif, "or they would not have been so easily taken by surprise. Why were they there? Their capture of the Cuban courier was accidental, I'm sure. They were on some other mission."

Last of all, the theft of the ship's boat and the strange behavior of the two Spaniards who had taken it and whom Clif had been forced to overcome added a peculiar feature to the affair.

Taking it all in all, Clif felt that though they had bravely avenged the murder of the Cuban, and had brought the dispatches safely to the rear admiral, and with them a prisoner, still an important object had not been accomplished.

He meant to return for that unexploded shell in the face of every difficulty and put his ideas to the test. He had this purpose in view when he delivered with his own hands the dispatches to the rear admiral.

Rear Admiral Sampson glanced quickly over the papers after they were handed to him, and seemed highly pleased.

"These are of the utmost importance," he exclaimed. "With this information we will be the better able to act in conjunction with the insurgents when the proper time comes."

Clif knew the papers must indeed be of especial value from the rear admiral's manner, for it was decidedly unusual for an officer of such importance to unbend to that extent with an ordinary cadet. The rear admiral was evidently more than satisfied with the result of Clif's mission.

After a hasty examination of the papers, he turned to Clif, who had remained standing, and asked some particulars of his meeting with the Cuban courier.

Then Clif briefly but graphically told of his receiving the papers from the hands of the insurgent and of the latter's tragic death so soon after at the hands of the cowardly Spanish soldier who held him as a prisoner of war.

Rear Admiral Sampson's blood fairly boiled as Clif gave him the details.

"The cowards!" he exclaimed, with clinched fist. "It was barbarous!"

"But, sir," continued Clif. "It has been avenged."

And then he briefly and with modest demeanor told of their attack upon the company of Spanish soldiers, and their victory over them without the loss of an American life. More than one Spaniard had gone to his death to atone for that cowardly assassination.

The rear admiral was plainly interested, and at his request Clif gave the particulars of his subsequent adventures and of the narrow escape in the boat from the Spanish soldiers firing upon them from the hill and shore.

"Admirable! admirable!" exclaimed the rear admiral, when the brief narrative was finished. "I am proud of the bravery of yourself and the men with you."

"And now, if you please, sir," said Clif, calmly, "I want to go back there."

"Back there!" exclaimed the admiral. "Where do you mean?"

"To the spot where I met the Cuban," replied Clif.

"What do you mean? According to your account the place is swarming with Spanish soldiers."

"Not many of them, sir," said Clif. "And it is not my intention that they should see me. I left something behind that I think is important."

Then he told of the shell that came crashing through the trees where they stood, and of the series of incidents that had prevented his examining it as fully as he wished.

He insisted strongly that the recovery of the shell was of the greatest importance, and intimated something of his ideas concerning the mystery that it suggested. He spoke to such good purpose that at last the rear admiral was disposed to grant his wish.

"But it would be better to wait until you have had a chance to rest a bit," said the latter. "To-morrow night, for instance."

"Delay is dangerous, sir, I think," said Clif. "Others are seeking it, I know, and it may not be there unless I go at once. There are still several hours of the night left, and I can easily accomplish it."

The rear admiral had evidently been impressed with what Clif had told him concerning the shell, and at last agreed that he should go about it in his own way.

"Very well, then," he said at last. "Take a boat's crew and go at once."

"If you please, sir," exclaimed Clif, "I would rather take one of the small boats and go alone. One man can move about with less fear of detection."

"Young man, you are undertaking a very dangerous mission," exclaimed the rear admiral. "But you seem to have the pluck, and I have confidence that you can take care of yourself. Do then as you wish, but take some signal rockets with you. Don't hesitate to use them if necessary. We will be ready to send you assistance if needed."

Clif, highly pleased at the confidence that was reposed in him, saluted respectfully and hastened away to prepare for the venture.

In a few minutes he was ready, the boat was lowered, and for the second time that night he left the flagship to face fresh dangers on the shore.

But this time he was alone. Success and safety depended upon his unaided efforts.

CHAPTER XXX.

THE BATTLE IN THE BRUSH.

Was it a foolhardy venture, he thought, as with steady stroke he forged ahead away from the flagship, and toward the shore he had so recently left amid the clatter of hostile bullets.

The enemy now must be on the alert, and he might be detected and captured the instant his boat touched shore. And he was not blind to the dangers that might confront him on land.

"I'm in for it now, at any rate," he thought, "and I've got to succeed. This mystery must be solved, and I believe the result will show that it is worth all the risk."

Darkness favored him, and besides he was alone; and for that very reason could move around with less risk of discovery once he reached land. He knew exactly where he had dropped the shell, and it would not take long to get it.

It was therefore with confidence that he urged the boat forward.

It was a long pull, for the flagship lay well out to sea, but Clif did not seem to feel the strain. He drew near the shore without detecting any hostile movement or hearing any sound that would lead him to think that the enemy were on the lookout.

He decided that it would be prudent not to land at the same spot as previously. He therefore steered for a clump of trees a little further down the coast, and still not a great distance from the hill where the shell lay.

Not a sound from the enemy reached his ears as his boat grated upon the sandy beach, and he sprang out to secure the painter to a bush.

Then, feeling that his revolver was ready and handy for business, he cautiously began to steal his way through the shrubbery that fringed the shore.

These screened his advance and soon he was ascending the steep bank in the direction of the previous encounter. He was getting further away from his boat and nearer and near to his destination.

"All serene, so far," he muttered, as he advanced steadily without any adventure. "The Spaniards must have gone."

But suddenly, as he was about to step from the concealment of the trees into a slight clearing that lay in his path, he heard a sound that caused him to dodge quickly back. Looking out he saw a figure close at hand and slowly approaching.

A step further and Clif would have brought himself directly within the other's view.

It was not Clif's purpose to invite an encounter, although he grasped his revolver in readiness for an emergency. He desired, rather, to avoid it, and to quietly make his way to the spot where the shell lay. That once secured, he felt that he could in the same way return to his boat and to the flagship.

He therefore silently waited in his place of concealment to see what the enemy would do. The latter evidently had not heard Clif's movements, and continued slowly to advance, stooping occasionally and peering from side to side.

"I think I know what you're after," muttered Clif below his breath. "But you won't find it here; nor me, either," he added, as he began to edge away from the position he held.

As he did so, the other turned and slowly continued his course in the opposite direction.

The coast was again clear, and Clif lost no time in putting what distance he could between himself and the unwelcome visitor. His course, too, led him toward the mound of earth behind which lay the object of his coming.

When he reached the spot where he had met the Cuban courier he found it deserted. The Spaniards, after the escape of Clif and his men, had evidently withdrawn.

With a light heart he sprang toward the rampart of earth and began to ascend its side.

"In one minute it is mine," he thought exultingly, "and then back to the flagship and the test!"

But a surprise was in store for him. As he vaulted over the top of the mound on to the other side, he landed almost into the arms of a man who was just ascending that side.

The man was unmistakably a Spaniard, and from his hands there fell a round shell, that rolled away across the ground.

The encounter was startling to both, but Clif was the first to recover his wits. His quick eye detected the fallen shell, and he divined the fellow's purpose.

Before the other could recover from his evident fright, Clif sprang upon him.

"So you have found it!" he muttered, as he closed in upon the Spaniard, "but finding's not keeping's this time."

Clif's attack brought the Spaniard quickly to his senses, and he was not slow to defend himself.

In a flash he drew his revolver, but Clif was too quick for him. The latter knocked the weapon from the fellow's grasp before he had a chance to fire it.

Clif's own weapon was within easy reach, but for several reasons he did not care to use it. He wanted, among other things, to avoid a pistol shot which might attract others to the spot.

The contest must be one of muscle against muscle; and to unusual strength Clif added a surprising agility that came in good stead in such a struggle.

They grappled, and there in that enclosure formed by the mounds of earth on several sides the two began a furious hand to hand battle, the result of which long hung in doubt.

The Spaniard was no mean opponent, and fought with enraged fury. Clif's astounding exertions during the past hours had been enough to exhaust the strongest and sturdiest, and he was compelled to acknowledge to himself, as the battle progressed, that it had made inroads upon his strength.

Back and forth across the little enclosure the pair fought fiercely. Once Clif slipped and fell beneath his opponent; but an instant after he was upon his feet.

His keen eye followed his antagonist's every move. He was watching for a chance to deliver one blow that would settle the combat. Several times he had landed upon the Spaniard's head and face, inflicting severe punishment, but not enough.

At last the moment came. The opening presented itself in the Spaniard's guard, and with all the strength that was in him, Clif shot out his right hand. It went home. With a force that seemed to lift the fellow high into the air, his fist met the Spaniard's chin, and the latter fell backward to the ground.

It was a clean knockout. Breathing heavily, the fellow lay where he had fallen, unconscious of his surroundings.

Clif was panting from the exertion. He had received some punishment, and the wound in his arm was throbbing fiercely.

But he paused only long enough to see that the fellow would not give him further trouble, and then hurried toward the spot where the shell had rolled.

"I guess that'll hold you for a while," he muttered, looking at his fallen foe as he started away.

"But he'll come out of it after a time," he added. "Gorry! how my arm aches all the way up to the elbow."

It took but a moment for him to find the shell, for he had seen it roll from the other's hand.

"That's it," he exclaimed, as he picked it up. "I'd know it in a minute by its shape and weight. Rather light for a cannon ball."

But he did not wait to examine it there. There would be time enough for that when he reached the flagship.

With a parting look at his unconscious antagonist he started away.

"I'm sorry, my dear sir," he exclaimed, sarcastically, as he looked back on reaching the top of the rampart. "You seemed so attached to this shell, I'd like to take you along with it. But as I can only take one at a time, I'll content myself with this."

Then he turned his back upon the scene of his contest, and started for his boat as expeditiously as due caution would allow.

He met with no obstacle in the way, and found the boat just as he had left it. He threw the shell in the stern, and with a feeling of exultation sprang in after it and seized the oars.

A few steady strokes and he was on the way toward the flagship. But there had been a change in those quiet waters while he was on the land.

He had not gone many boat lengths from shore before he discovered looming up before him a slowly moving steamer. It was apparently hugging the coast and proceeding with as little noise as possible.

"A boat trying to run the blockade!" exclaimed Clif, as he backed water and rested upon his oars. "She'll succeed, too, unless one of our ships should happen to discover her with its searchlight."

And then his responsibility, in view of the discovery he had made, flashed upon him.

"I must warn the flagship at once," he exclaimed, seizing the oars and sending the boat forward with a spurt.

But after a couple of strokes he suddenly stopped again.

"What a fool I am!" he exclaimed. "By the time I can row out to the flagship, it will be too late. They must be warned instantly, and there is only one way of doing it."

He reached for the signal rockets he had brought at the rear admiral's order. Should he fire them?

Those on board the strange boat that was nearly abreast of him did not know that he was there. If he gave the signal it would betray his presence, and no doubt lead to an attack upon himself in his open boat.

Clif looked far out to sea for a moment, half hoping to see the flash of the searchlight play upon the water, and lead to the detection of the strange craft.

But the delay was only momentary.

"It is my duty to warn the ships," he exclaimed, as he set a rocket up in the stern, and drawing a match from his pocket, struck it upon the seat of the boat. "Here goes!"

A moment later, with a sharp whirr and a flash of light, the rocket shot up into the air. A second and third followed; then Clif sprang back upon his seat and seized the oars.

The signal had been given. He had done his duty at whatever risk there might be to his own safety.

CHAPTER XXXI.

CAPTURED.

Clif had elected to imperil his own existence rather than allow one of the enemy's boats to pass that blockade without warning to the American ships. But he had no intention of lying idly by in the path of the hostile craft.

He waited but a moment after the glare of the last rocket had died out in the air, and then bent to the oars, and urged the boat toward the open sea beyond.

And then he had every confidence that he had little to fear from the enemy's boat.

"They'll have all they can do to look out for their own safety now," he thought, "without paying any attention to me. The New York has seen the signal, and will not be slow in making out the cause. Then look out, Mr. Spaniard."

But there was more taking place upon those waters than Clif was cognizant of, and peril came from an unlooked-for source.

His decision to send up the warning signal had been quickly formed after his first discovery of the strange vessel. He had seen at a glance that it was not a warship, but a merchant steamer. It was moving slowly, and apparently seeking, as much as possible, the concealment afforded by the shadow of the coast. Every feature about it showed that it was trying to quietly steal out past the blockading vessels.

Clif had not delayed, but on the impulse of the moment had sent up the signal rockets while he was yet between the ship and the shore. But a few steady strokes would carry him beyond the enemy and toward the flagship, he thought.

But to his surprise he noticed, on glancing over his shoulder as he drew nearer the vessel, that the latter was moving slower than before and in fact had just stopped.

This was puzzling to him, for now, if at any time, the boat should be showing its utmost speed. Those on board must surely know from the signals that they had been discovered and that pursuit would instantly follow.

A few words will explain the situation to the reader. The vessel was, as Clif suspected, endeavoring to steal out past the American ships, which were known to be in the vicinity. But a short time before Clif had left the shore for the second time, the blockade runner had slowed down, and a boat, manned by half a dozen sailors, had been sent ashore. An officer in the Spanish army, with important dispatches, was to be taken aboard at a point not far from where Clif had landed.

The work of the Spanish boat's crew had been expeditiously performed, and when Clif sent up his signal, they were returning to the ship. Unnoticed by Clif in his excitement at the time, they were close to one side of his boat at that fateful moment.

A pistol shot suddenly ringing out in the air and a bullet flying not far from his head apprised the cadet of danger from that quarter. The Spaniards, as was natural for them to be, were aroused to a high pitch of excitement against the youth whose vigilance promised to set all their plans at naught.

With a hoarse yell of rage they tugged at the oars and their boat fairly leaped through the water after the intrepid young cadet.

Clif saw the movement, and redoubled his efforts at the oars. It was a race for his life—one against seven!

With frantic energy he tugged at the oars, and his boat shot forward with encouraging speed. At that moment the searchlight on the flagship sent its rays across the waters in answer to the signal, and a dazzling stream of light played upon the scene.

It brought in clear relief the form of the waiting steamer, and the two boats racing so desperately near at hand.

What a thrilling scene it must have been to the officers on the bridge of the flagship as with glass in hand they watched the exciting race. But it was not given to them long to note the cadet's desperate struggle for freedom, or to marvel at his great endurance.

The race was a short one, and the result a foregone conclusion. There was no hope of Clif's escaping from the pursuing boat, with its crew of fresh and eager oarsmen. The latter closed in upon him with a leap and a bound, and soon were within oar's length of him.

He recognized the uselessness of trying to escape from them, but was determined not to surrender without a struggle even in the face of great numbers.

He dropped his oars and sprang to his feet, facing his enemies. He drew his revolver, but before he could use it one of the Spanish sailors, who had risen in the boat, knocked it from his grasp with his oar.

The boats were now side by side, almost touching, and the dark hulk of the steamer was not many feet away.

From the latter arose aloud cheer as they saw that Clif had been disarmed, and above the noise Clif could hear a few words of command from the Spanish army officer who sat in the stern of the boat at his side. It was to the sailor who had sprung up to attack Clif.

"Don't shoot!" he said. "Take him alive!"

Clif had seized an oar when his revolver fell with a splash into the water, and there was no doubt that he intended using it.

But two can play at that game, and the Spanish sailor, forbidden to shoot, attacked Clif furiously with the oar, which he still held in his hand.

Clif dodged, but as he did so another sailor aimed a blow at his head. The aim was good.

A sharp pain shot through the young cadet's head, he reeled and all became dark before him. With a faint moan he fell senseless into the bottom of his boat.

The contest had been short, and well it was for the Spaniards that such was the case. Already the flickering of the searchlight told that the flagship was hurrying to the scene.

The Spaniards realized the importance of quick action. They had, on the impulse of the moment, retaliated upon Clif because it could take but a few minutes and because they felt that the chase would end not far from their waiting vessel.

They congratulated themselves that it had, indeed, brought them almost to the ship's side, and now they lost no time in getting themselves and their prisoner aboard. Willing hands assisted from above.

A couple of strokes of the oars had brought them to the ship's side, with Clif's boat in tow. In obedience to a command, Clif's boat with its unconscious burden was raised bodily to the deck. The captain thought he could use it in his business.

A moment later the Spaniards with the army officer reached the deck, and the ship's captain signaled to go ahead.

All now was excitement on board the Spaniard. Beyond securely fastening the arms and legs of their unconscious captive where he lay, they paid but little attention to Clif. They were all too wrapped up in thoughts of escape from the cruiser whose piercing searchlight was streaming upon them.

Among the crew there was, here and there, a murmur against the delay that had been caused by stopping to take on the army officer, and with this was coupled a note of resentment against the young cadet whose appearance on the scene promised to spoil all their plans.

But the captain's orders were carried out promptly, the more so as their own safety depended upon it.

They were not without hope of making good their escape in the end, for they knew what speed their craft was capable of. It was a fast boat, and the throbbing of the engines told that she was being urged to her full speed.

Amid intense excitement of crew and officers, the wild dash for freedom and safety had begun.

Through all this confusion and flurry the cadet whose prompt signaling had occasioned it lay helpless and unconscious. The steady thump of the machinery below, which was steadily carrying him further and further from his friends, made no impression upon his ears, nor was his mind aroused by the excitement of the chase or the hope of rescue.

But the race had not been long under way before he began to show signs of returning consciousness. He stirred uneasily in the bottom of the boat where he lay, attempting to move his pinioned limbs; then a long-drawn breath, and he opened his eyes slowly.

The noise from shipboard fell upon his ears, and the sounds confused him. His surroundings puzzled him and his mind at first could not grasp the situation. Where was he?

Then with a rush of recollection came the remembrance of the attack upon him in the open boat. His enemies had triumphed, he thought, and left him a helpless victim to drift about upon the open sea. But whence those sounds?

He painfully raised himself to a sitting posture and looked out. To his astonishment, he found himself and boat upon the deck of a swiftly moving steamer.

Then he saw it all, and realized what had happened. He caught a glimpse of the rays of the searchlight that still streamed across the water, and a moment after heard the boom of a cannon out at sea.

"The New York!" he exclaimed. "She is in pursuit! But she's too far away, and can never catch this fast boat. The only chance of her stopping it is with one of her big guns."

And then, involuntarily, he shuddered as he thought that, bound and helpless, he would share the fate of the Spanish crew if a shot from the flagship should penetrate the ship's side and send it to the bottom!

He moved a little toward the stern of his boat, as best he could, to get a better view of the light that showed the approaching flagship. As he did so he struck a round, hard object that lay behind him.

"The unexploded shell!" he exclaimed, as he recognized what it was. "I still have that with me, at any rate!"

And then he began to tug at the ropes that bound his arms in a frantic effort to loosen them.

The rapid throb of the engines below and another boom of cannon from out to sea told that the chase was becoming a hot one.

CHAPTER XXXII.

CLIF FARADAY'S TEST.

The excitement among the crew of the Spanish steamer was intense as they watched the light from the flagship and noted the course of the projectiles that came toward them. For this reason they had not observed Clif's movements, and gave themselves no concern about him.

Whatever may have been his intended course of action, he was at last compelled to abandon it.

Strain and tug as he would at the cords that bound his arms, they remained intact, nor could his ingenuity devise any way of releasing himself from their hold. Though hastily tied, the knots had been put there to stay, and Clif at last realized that it was a hopeless task to try to undo them.

But though he could not free his arms and legs, he could use his eyes, and the scene was one thrilling enough to rivet his attention.

The fast moving steamer, urged to its utmost speed, the exclamations of hope and fear among its crew, the more majestically moving flagship whose deficiencies of speed were more than atoned for by the range of her guns, suggested possibilities to one in Clif's position that might well set one's heart to beating wildly.

If the steamer should escape by reason of superior speed, it would bring joy to the crew, but disaster to Clif, their helpless prisoner. If, on the other hand, a shot from the flagship should sink the Spanish boat, Clif perforce would share death with them. Little wonder that brave as he was, he struggled anxiously to free his arms and legs from their bonds.

"The New York can never catch us," he exclaimed, when he had settled down to watching the flagship as best he could. "She is too far away, and this boat is too fast."

There was little need of the searchlight now, as dawn was approaching. The forms of the ships could be distinguished in the uncertain light without its aid.

Clif had been watching the flagship which was astern, but now, looking forward, he saw a beam of light in that direction. It was several miles out to sea, and shot across their path.

"That must be the Wilmington," he exclaimed, cheered by a suddenly revived hope. "She can cut across our path, and all may yet be well."

He looked back at the flagship and saw the red and the blue signal lights flashing their message to the ship ahead which was, as Clif surmised, the Wilmington. They also carried a message to Clif, nor was their meaning lost upon the Spanish crew.

"They have signaled the Wilmington to intercept her," exclaimed Clif. "But it will be a close race."

He heard the signal from the excited captain of the Spanish boat for more speed, and the throbbing of the machinery told that they were endeavoring in the engine rooms to carry out the order. It seemed as if the engines were already doing their utmost, but Clif could notice a slight increase in the headway they were making.

It was a fast boat and no mistake, Clif thought, as he anxiously strained his eyes to see what the Wilmington was doing.

Answering signals told that she had received the order from the flagship, and that those orders would be obeyed. Clif fervently hoped that she would be successful. He hated to think of the possibility of a hostile ship succeeding in running the blockade, and now this patriotic impulse was heightened by the fact that he was a helpless prisoner on board the very boat that promised to accomplish that feat.

For, as he watched the race, there was a growing conviction in Clif's mind that the Wilmington was so far out to sea that she could not hope to stop the Spanish steamer except by the power of her guns. And a hole in the side of the enemy's vessel, however desirable under ordinary circumstances, did not coincide with his hopes or ideas on this occasion. He had no desire to share a watery grave with his captors.

The two boats were heading for the same point, the Wilmington seeking to block the path the other was following. One of her guns spoke out, but the shot fell short. She was not in range.

Faster went the Spanish boat, and nearer to the objective point raced the two vessels.

Clif breathlessly watched the pursuing craft whose success meant so much to him. Could she win?

The Spaniards shared his excitement, and watched their opponent with fully as much eagerness. At last they broke out into a cheer.

Clif was not slow to understand its import. The Spanish boat was making really a phenomenal run, and had reached a point where it was evident that if they maintained their speed they would soon be past the dangerous line. That once reached they could show the Yankee boat a clean pair of heels.

Clif's spirits fell when he realized that the Spaniards had good cause for their jubilation. There was no doubt now that the steamer could pass the danger line and then away.

The Wilmington, too, seemed to realize that there was no hope of catching up with the other vessel, for now the cannon boomed out in rapid succession. They were rapidly drawing nearer and within range.

A shot swept across the Spaniard's bows, but on she went. Then another struck the bridge upon which the captain stood glass in hand, and he had a narrow escape from flying splinters. But the goal was too near for them to stop, and he signaled for more steam.

Clif could not but admire this officer's pluck. Under other circumstances, he would have said that the Spaniard deserved to win.

The vessel seemed to struggle to do what was demanded of her, and sped on. Another shot from the Wilmington rattled across her bows, but the crew answered with a cheer. Five minutes more and they would be round the point and then——

What would happen then was never to be known. Suddenly a loud explosion was heard from below, and the whole frame of the steamer shook from end to end. Men rushed on deck in a panic, and wildly proclaimed the cause.

A steam pipe, urged beyond its strength, had exploded, carrying destruction with it. The race was lost, and the captain promptly hauled down his flag.

But as he did so, he gave orders to steer toward the land, and the steamer came to a standstill not far from the shore.

The Spanish army officer carrying the dispatches entered a boat that was quickly lowered and when the prize crew from the Wilmington boarded the steamer he was safe upon land and his escape was assured.

When the officer in charge of the prize crew had finished the formalities, Clif attracted his attention. The cadet had apparently been forgotten by his captors in the excitement of the chase and the calamity that had come upon them. The American officer was astonished beyond measure to find one wearing the familiar uniform in such a plight on that boat.

"Why, Mr. Faraday," he exclaimed upon learning Clif's identity, and having released him from his bonds, "we were not aware that they had an American on board as a prisoner."

"I thought not, from the way you were firing at us," said Clif, with a smile. "I thought more than once that you would send this particular American to the bottom along with the shipload of the enemy. You were firing too accurately to suit me this time."

"Well, the American boys do come pretty near hitting what they aim at," responded the officer, evidently pleased at the compliment to their marksmanship. "But I am curious to know how it has happened that we find you here."

Clif then briefly told of the adventures that followed his finding of the unexploded shell, which he picked up from its lodgment in the boat and held in his hand.

"So you have risked your life for that piece of steel!" exclaimed the officer. "What can have been your purpose in that?"

"Does it not strike you, sir, that there is something peculiar about it?" asked Clif, as the other examined it.

"Yes," replied the officer, "it is decidedly out of date, and might be interesting as a relic, but not of sufficient importance to risk one's life for."

"I had an idea that there was a mystery about it that was well worth solving," replied Clif. "And with your permission, sir, I will put the matter to a test."

"As you like," responded the officer, with the air of a man who is indulging some childish fancy.

Clif was not slow to take advantage of the permission granted, and carried the shell to a table that stood upon the after deck, the officer meantime paying no further attention to him, but attending to some further detail of transfer.

Clif had procured a fuse and inserted it into the shell and was upon the point of lighting it when the officer appeared.

"Stop, sir!" he commanded. "Would you blow us all to destruction?"

Others standing near made a move as if to stop Clif, but it was too late. The fuse was burning rapidly.

With a cry of alarm and amazement, the officers, American as well as Spanish, sprang to one side and dodged in great fright.

But Clif calmly stood by, his arms folded and a confident smile playing about his lips.

He was putting his theory to the test.

CHAPTER XXXIII.

THE MYSTERY OF THE UNEXPLODED SHELL.

Mingled with evident fright and alarm there was upon the face of each a look of incredulity at rashness of the cadet. Had his adventures and narrow escapes turned his brain, and were they now at the mercy of a maniac? was in the minds of all.

They had not long to wait. The fuse burned rapidly and spluttered to the end, and as they all involuntarily ducked their heads at the impending explosion, a peculiar thing happened.

When the fire from the fuse reached the shell there was a sharp clicking sound, and those who were looking at the shell saw it suddenly open like a book, and from its hollow interior fell a roll of paper upon the table.

This Clif seized and waved over his head in triumph.

"Hurrah!" he cried. "It is as I suspected. Secret dispatches from the enemy that are worth all they have cost!"

The officers were struck dumb with amazement, and stood and stared at the smiling young man as though they could not believe their eyes. But after a time they crowded around him and examined the shell curiously, and then the papers that Clif held in his hand.

The papers were evidently written in Spanish, and though the American officers could not read them, they now had conceived sufficient confidence in Clif to believe that they were indeed of importance.

The shell, whose quest had caused Clif so much peril and danger, was a curious affair. It had been cunningly contrived for the purpose it had so admirably fulfilled. Though very much in appearance like the old-fashioned round shells, it was in two parts, ingeniously hinged so that when closed it required very close scrutiny to detect the seam.

It was hollow, and consequently light in weight. This fact had first arrested Clif's attention and had set his thoughts to work upon the mystery that was connected with it. In the opening where the fuse was inserted there was a concealed mechanism so arranged that it might not be detected or opened with the finger, but would readily give way to the force of a slight explosion in that small cavity. If it should fall into strange hands, unfamiliar with its design, it was meant to defy all efforts at opening it.

Clif was the recipient of many expressions of praise from the American officers upon his ingenuity in fathoming the secret that was so cunningly devised, and they questioned him at length.

"That is indeed wonderful," said the superior officer. "But how did you ever guess the purpose for which it was intended or the method of opening it?"

Clif then explained the circumstances connected with its appearance at his feet among the trees where he was awaiting the Cuban courier.

"I thought it was strange that a ship being pursued should fire a shell at the land instead of at its enemy," he said, "and when I picked it up I was struck with its peculiarities, but my examination was interrupted by the arrival of the Spanish soldiers. We were kept busy for a while pursuing them, and did not have much time to pursue this mystery."

The officer smiled knowingly at this, for he had gathered enough from Clif's previous narrative to know that the little band of sailors had done great feats that night.

"The shell not exploding," continued Clif, "led me to think that perhaps it was not intended to explode just then and when I saw that the Spanish soldiers seemed to be hunting for something there, I jumped to the conclusion that it was this identical piece of steel they were after. That explained their presence there and their peculiar behavior. And what could the Spaniards want with that shell if it did not contain something of value to them and of greater value to the American cause?"

"You reasoned well," exclaimed the officer, "and so you decided to risk going back for it, and your ideas have come out triumphant through the test. But, young man, don't try any more experiments like that when I'm around."

They all laughed heartily at this sally, at which Clif joined in.

"But it was decidedly a peculiar way to send dispatches," continued the officer, "and it would seem as though it was uncertain and unnecessary as well."

"There seemed to me to be a good reason for it, sir," said Clif. "I figured that that boat had been sent to deliver the dispatches, with instructions that if they were pursued to fire the shell at a point agreed upon, and then make their escape. They were pursued, and did fire toward shore, and the soldiers in waiting evidently saw the flash, and knew about where to hunt for it. I think, sir, that when these papers are examined it will be found that they contain information that the Spanish army ashore wants the worst way."

This proved to be the case. Clif was given custody of the peculiar shell and the papers it had contained, and after a little delay was taken in the boat to the Wilmington.

Signals were exchanged between this vessel and the flagship, and in due time Clif was rowed to the latter and ordered to report to the rear admiral.

He turned the shell and its contents over to that officer with an explanation of all that had taken place.

"I see that you had good cause for desiring to go back to find this shell," said the rear admiral when Clif had finished. "We have learned from the prisoner whom you secured after a struggle in your boat, that they had stolen your boat to facilitate the transfer of some papers. They were late and missed seeing the boat that fired this shell. Now that you have secured these papers I will call your knowledge of Spanish into requisition and allow you to transcribe these for me."

And this Clif did; and when he had completed the task it was found that the most important work he had done that night, was in securing that shell and unraveling its mystery.

As he issued from the admiral's room Cadet Wells, one of Clif's best friends, approached him.

"Faraday, old fellow," he said, "I've got news that will interest you."

"I'm listening."

"It's about that exception among Spaniards, the lieutenant who helped you and Miss Stuart escape."

"Ah! what of him?" asked Clif, eagerly.

"You know he left us on a Spanish boat that brought you over under a flag of truce. Well, we couldn't touch that boat then, of course, but yesterday she ventured too far out, and the New York sunk her. We saved all her crew and from one of them I learned what became of Hernandez. It seems he sought a lonely part of the boat while she was on the way from us to the shore, and knelt to pray. An officer of the boat saw him thus and withdrew. A moment later all hands were startled by a pistol shot. Hurrying below they found Lieutenant Hernandez prone on the deck, a calm smile on his face, a bullet in his brain."

Faraday was deeply affected.

"And thus," he said gravely, "perished one of Spain's real heroes."

[THE END.]

Milton Keynes UK
Ingram Content Group UK Ltd.
UKHW030624061024
449204UK00004B/341